HOLLYWOOD AND LE VINE

Hollywood and LeVine

by *ANDREW BERGMAN*

HOLT, RINEHART AND WINSTON

NEW YORK

Copyright © 1975 by Andrew Bergman
All rights reserved, including the right
to reproduce this book or portions thereof in any form.
Published simultaneously in Canada
by Holt, Rinehart and Winston of Canada, Limited.
Library of Congress Cataloging in Publication Data
Bergman, Andrew.
  Hollywood and LeVine.

  I. Title.
PZ4.B4978Ho   [PS3552.E7193]   813'.5'4   74–15472
ISBN 0–03–013816–7
First Edition
Printed in the United States of America

In sweet memory
of another writer,
my father,
Rudy Bergman

HOLLYWOOD AND LEVINE

PROLOGUE

The postwar years were great for private detectives. Never better, before or since. You would not believe how many soldiers contacted shamuses, strictly on the q.t., to find out what their little women had been doing to keep busy during the big war. The saloons of New York were packed with GIs day and night, big shots for a year, telling watery-eyed Paddy how the French girls had frenched them, the German girls had blitzed them, and the English girls had squeezed out their tea bags. Then they would leave the saloons and call up guys like me, suddenly fearful that their wives and fiancées, like they, had used the war to sample some of the local talent.

I charged twenty-five bucks to run a check and could have gotten double that, that's how desperate these guys were, how hungry for reassurance. And reassurance is what they generally got. Keep this under your hat, but half the time I didn't actually investigate. What for? Either the marriage held up or it didn't. Why cripple the guy's ego and sense of well-being? He had problems enough re-adjusting to the States. And what is infidelity in such a situation? Frankie is overseas, his picture is on the bureau, and Millie pines away, looking at the clock and wondering what time it is in Bastogne. Is Frankie getting the hotfoot from the Nazis or maybe the Lucky Pierre from a couple of local milkmaids? And it's Christmas Eve and the doorbell rings and who's there but Jerry, Frankie's 4-F pal from the old neighborhood, standing in the doorway with a friendly smile, a fresh haircut, and a bottle of scotch wrapped up bright and ribbony for the holidays. His coat smells fresh and cold from the outside and he's such a good friend. So they talk about things—hear from Frankie? —and pretty soon come the tears and more scotch and then comforting hugs, leading to some tentative then ferocious, leg-twisting necking, and finally a round of miserable sex. More tears, the evening ends, and Millie has been, at least officially, unfaithful. But if that's infidelity then I'm Dana Andrews.

I'm not. I'm Jack LeVine, a private dick with the wise and forgiving heart of a Talmudic sage. So when the war ends and Frankie calls up, asking me to check on Millie and please don't tell anyone, I do absolutely nothing. Two days later I call him back and tell him that Millie is a girl to be proud of. Welcome home, soldier, job well done, your wife's twat is cobwebbed with disuse. Nobody's hurt, everybody breathes easier, sleeps better, and steps livelier, and I've made another easy twenty-five.

By 1947, however, the soldiers were working out their own problems and my bank account was shrinking back to normal. I dug into my wall safe one afternoon and came out with a fistful of dust, rusting paper clips, and small American and Canadian change. The party was over and it wasn't any fun because it looked to me like the rest of New York was dancing cheek to cheek and tipping the maestro to play another. For reasons intimately connected to life, death, and feelings of immortality occasioned by the simple act of walking unaided off a troop ship, a binge was in progress. Everything was crowds, lines, and shortages, yet people continued to choke the streets, looking for ways to spend their money. New York being what it is, they were not disappointed.

Day life, night life, morning life, whatever; all were marked by crowds straining against barricades. The monkeys who held the red velvet ropes at the Copa and Latin Quarter were making more money than Truman; getting a decent table required signing over your house, life insurance, and matched luggage. Good and bad restaurants were filled and smoky all the time and you couldn't get near the Stadium no matter who the Yankees were playing.

Apartments were not to be found anywhere, but if you managed to spot one, it meant stuffing the superintendent's pockets with gold bullion and treasury notes just to get a look-see. I know people who bought the early editions, scanned the obituaries, and then hailed cabs directly to the deceased's apartment building. Before the relatives had even found a comfortable place to sit shiva, strangers were wandering through the rooms and poking around in closets. It was gruesome, it was terrible, yet even the mourners understood. Life was transitory, but apartments were forever; the fortresses that bordered Central Park and West End and Park avenues were built for a thousand years.

The apartment shortage was like a lot of shortages rolled into one. There was a shortage of roots, a shortage of stability, a shortage of knowing what the hell to do with your life. All the drinking and shouting and pushing your way into the Stork Club didn't fool LeVine: the end of the war wasn't a relief, it was a big goddamn letdown. After the soldiers combed the confetti out of their hair, they sat down and commenced to brood. People had no time for heroes after the first couple of months of parades and Sunday spreads. But the heroes had time by the clock-load. They were unprepared for this peace, for its lack of majesty. Face it, working and riding the subways were just nothing at all after chasing Hitler and Tojo around the world, after liberating villages in flower-strewn jeeps. With the enemy vanquished, what was left to give purpose to a life? The GIs became displaced persons.

So crowded taxis headed for crowded bars and the GIs stood six deep around the rail and told lies to each other. Sometimes I listened. They were confused, they had schemes, they were optimists, they were hurt. They had seen too many dead and reeking bodies to ever really become civilians again. Their notions of making a living were grandiose and laced with get-rich-quick; their speech was filled with remembered pain and booze-soaked visions of the future as a perfect, glistening soap bubble.

It was pretty innocent thinking, but it looks good to me now. At least the war was over and it had been won. I can't think, offhand, of what we've won since. And that time, right after the war, was the last really optimistic period for a good long while. In February of 1947, my fondness for that period and its eccentricities came to an end. It went all sour and wrong for me.

Enter Walter Adrian, screenwriter.

Walter Adrian had been nominated for Academy Awards in 1937 and 1942, for two pictures you've probably heard of—*Three-Star Extra* and *Beloved Heart*. The first of the two was a funny and noisy film about an ace reporter busting open a crime ring and getting himself a fat raise and a paid vacation. There was a lot of shooting and fast cars and dumb cops: my kind of picture. *Beloved Heart* was about a beautiful young school teacher dying of a dread and nameless disease, the kind that manifests itself in very white skin and very long speeches. I saw it at the Roxy, amid so much sobbing I thought I had wandered into a funeral, a funeral that had been unaccountably preceded by a stage show. I hated the picture, hated Walter for writing it, and hated myself for paying to see it. It treated death like something you see in an Easter egg and death isn't like that; it's nasty and inconvenient and enormous.

Anyhow, Walter had gotten the nominations but not the actual Oscars. He didn't really deserve to. His other distinction was that he had been my classmate and friend at the City College of New York, and unlike myself, had gone on to graduate. He became a newspaper reporter and then a scenario writer. I became a guy who lived in Sunnyside, Queens. And now, in 1947, on Valentine's Day, we hooked up professionally because Walter Adrian thought he was being followed.

It had been years since Adrian and I had last spoken. There was no rift, nothing that dramatic, just the inevitable drifting apart of friends living completely different kinds of lives. I left school in 1927 and Walter got his diploma in '28. He worked for the *Daily News* for four years, during which time we frequently had lunch at the Old Seidelburg, on Third Avenue, a newsman's hangout. In 1932, he sold a story to Paramount Pictures and took a train out West to see what Hollywood was all about. He saw and never took the train back. We corresponded irregularly, then not at all. In 1940, I ran into Adrian on Fifth Avenue. He was wearing a camel's-hair coat and a tweed cap, looking well-barbered and content and every inch the successful young writer. The woman he was with wasn't half-bad either, but I don't think she was in the literary line. Adrian had hugged me and pounded my back; he asked for my number and said we'd have to get together soon, to down some dark beer and talk about the old days.

Seven years later we got together. It was late afternoon of Valentine's Day and I sat in my Broadway office typing a dreary report on the tailing of an Argentinian importer named Carlos Teitelbaum. I heard the outer office door open and close and looked up to see Adrian standing uncertainly in the reception area, holding a gray fedora in his hands.

"Jack?" he said tentatively. Then he grinned. "Hey, Baldy."

"Well, Walter of Hollywood," I called out. "Come in, take a number."

Adrian walked shyly into the inner office and I rose to greet him. He didn't pound my back this time, just shook my hand and sank wearily into the overstuffed chair that faces my desk. He looked pretty awful. His thin, angular face was drawn and gray, the blue eyes had gone glassy, his slightly oversized mouth was slack and glum. Walter was wearing his black hair long; it curled around his ears and reached his shirt collar. He caught me looking and smoothed the hair back with his hands.

"Don't say it. I look lousy."

"You look lousy. How come?"

He shrugged. "Events. You haven't changed a bit though, Jack. Honestly, you're looking wonderful. When did we last see each other, before the war?"

"1940. On Fifth Avenue, in front of Saks. It was Christmas and you had a bunch of packages, including a blond one. Very nice, I remember."

Adrian didn't. "1940?" It came to him. "Oh, *her*." He smiled to himself, well-satisfied. "A starlet."

"I figured."

"It was after my first marriage. I'm married again, you know. To an incredible girl, Helen. She's almost ten years younger than I am, thirty-one, but so much wiser." Talking about her brought some color back to his face. "Weren't you married when I saw you?"

"Kind of. But no more."

"What happened?"

I didn't feel like telling him, or hearing it myself. Being married to a private dick is no fun; it's dangerous and the money stinks. It starts with bickering, then it gets worse than that.

"Events," I said.

"Okay. Just curious."

"It's not all that interesting. Your basic falling-apart. Coffee?"

He said he'd love some, then lit up some kind of foreign cigarette with an aroma akin to what you might get off a weight lifter's jockstrap. He puffed on it and yawned. I poured out two cups of java, handed him his, and drew a Lucky out of my shirt pocket. We sipped and puffed in silence, as if paying our respects to the memory of our friendship. It was a strained moment: we really didn't know each other anymore.

Walter must have been thinking the same thing.

"Long time, huh, Jack?"

"Long time, Walter." I stared out my window, across the airshaft. The clerks at Fidelity Insurance stood at the files, eyes on the clock, winding down another day of pointless employment. I spun back around in my chair.

"You going to tell me what the problem is, Walter, or am I supposed to tease it out of you?"

Adrian blinked and looked annoyed, not at me, I think, but at the fact that he had a problem at all. He leaned forward and tapped his cigarette into an ashtray I had stolen from El Morocco.

"I'm being followed, Jack. All over New York." He raised his head from the ashtray. "What do you make of that?"

"A pair of socks. What do you mean, what I do make of it? Nothing. I've got to have a little background. The pertinent questions are for how long, why, and by whom?"

Adrian sat back in the chair and shook his head. "I wish I could answer you, Jack. Who and why I draw a complete blank on; how long is about four days."

"When did you get into town?"

"A week ago." He remembered his etiquette. "I meant to call you, Jack, socially. For dinner . . ."

I held up my hand.

"Spare me, Walter. This is a business call."

"Business—friendship. I came to you because you know me and I know you. We can level with each other. We can trust each other."

"Check. We're both great guys. Why are you in New York?"

He crossed his legs; the right one started jiggling. "I wrote a play, *Destiny's Stepson*." He smiled before I could say a word. "I know the title stinks, but it's a good play.

8

Returning soldier confronts family. Obviously, I want to get it produced here. I've been meeting with some money men. So far, no dice."

"No dice? For a hotshot screenwriter? That's hard to believe."

"It's not so unusual. Theater people in the East look down on screenwriters. They resent the kind of money we make and take it out on us professionally. They claim we can't write seriously, that we've been compromised forever."

"And that's why you can't find a backer for your play?"

Adrian shifted in his seat, looking glum. "It's the only reason that makes any sense to me," he said, knitting his fingers together.

"How about some reasons that don't make any sense," I said. "You got any of those?"

"No." It was a cold and final "no," the kind that generally precedes "trespassing."

"Fair enough," I told Adrian. The hell with it, there was no sense pushing him. "What do you want from me?"

"Find out why I'm being followed."

"You don't have a clue?"

"None whatsoever," he said flatly.

"Ex-wife, anything like that? Think hard, Walter. I'm not trying to be nosey, it's just that a tail can have its source in something you might think trivial or forgotten."

He pretended to think about it, then shook his head vigorously.

"Nope, Jack. As for my ex-wife, she got alimony, and plenty of it, for three years. Then she remarried. No reason for her to have any interest in my affairs."

I beat out a little Krupa time on the top of my desk. Adrian was as communicative as a toilet seat, but I didn't think he was holding out on me for any malicious reason. That's what bothered me: it's the ones with good intentions who get you pushed off the tops of buildings.

"What you're basically asking from me, then, is to tail the guy who's tailing you, find out who's paying him, and why."

"That sounds about right," Walter said vaguely. He was thinking about something else as he said it, then stood up abruptly. "You busy tonight, Jack?"

"No."

"How about dinner at Lindy's, six-thirty? I just want to get back to the hotel and take a shower." His eyes were pleading for a yes so I gave it to him.

"Six-thirty it is."

I walked Adrian to the door. He opened it and suddenly gripped my upper arm.

"Jack, if I made a big mistake, would you still go to bat for me?"

"Depends on the mistake and on the bat."

He smiled and his eyes relaxed. For the first time since he had arrived, Adrian was in the same room with me.

"I knew you would," he said, and left.

I went back to my desk and stuck my feet up on the windowsill. The clerks at Fidelity were getting their coats and lining up at the time clock. I felt a familiar pang and wished for nothing more complicated than to punch out with them and ride the subway home to the wife, kids, and leaping pooch. Dinner, the sports pages, radio, yell at the kids a little, and bed down with my gentle and obliging missus. Not big demands, just impossible ones.

I watched the clerks file out and wondered about the possible dimensions of Walter Adrian's mistake, pretty sure that I was getting into another ungodly mess.

Adrian had gotten there ahead of me and was waiting in front of Lindy's, taller than most of the people who swept past him into the restaurant. It was a surprising night for February, mild and wet and gusty; the screenwriter's hair was blowing about wildly and he stood tightly wrapped in his raincoat, like a ship's captain in an epic storm.

"Why didn't you wait inside?" I asked him.

Adrian just shrugged and we pushed through the revolving doors into the brightly lit interior. Lindy's was a famous hangout for show business types, gamblers, and dress manufacturers who thought they fit into the first two categories. The cheesecake was legendary, but I did not really like Lindy's at all; it was full of comedians, professional and amateur, who belittled each other and pretended it was done out of affection. The camaraderie and warmth was as genuine as an electric hearth.

We got a booth near the back and ordered a couple of drinks. Adrian looked better, having shaved, changed, and freshened up.

"Where did you leave him?" I asked.

"Leave who?"

"The tail."

Our drinks arrived. The fat gray-haired waiter wanted to know if we were ready to order. When we said no, he grunted and walked away.

We clinked glasses.

"To old friendship renewed," said Adrian, his eyes glittering. He seemed very happy.

"To crime," I replied, delicately sipping my iced bourbon. "The tail, Walter, where did you leave him?"

"There isn't any tail, Jack. I made that up before."

He opened up his menu and studied it.

"No tail," I said quietly, as if to confirm it. I was surprised and not surprised. "You want to explain why you told me you were being followed, Walter?"

Adrian wouldn't lift his eyes from the menu.

"Don't be angry, Jack. I do need your help." He finally looked up. "But I couldn't just come in off the street and spill. I had to see how I felt with you, had to chat and get comfortable. Trust is very important in something like this."

"Like what?"

"Like what I need you for. When you asked what the problem was, I said the first thing that sounded plausible.

Being followed sprang to mind. I used it in *Murder Street*."
He smiled. "Fooled you."

"That's not so hard."

The waiter returned and wouldn't leave until we ordered.
Walter and I both opted for the brisket. The waiter tore the
menus from our hands and departed.

"Okay, Walter, for real this time: what's the problem?"

The writer finished off his manhattan and coughed a bit,
his cheeks flushing red. Then he folded his hands before
him.

"It's kind of a long story," he began. "The background,
that is."

"There aren't any short stories in my business."

"So you'll be patient?"

"I'm even patient with strangers, Walter."

He was moved by the remark. His eyes went a little wet
and he nodded.

"I know, Jack. That's why I'm talking to you." Adrian
rubbed the corners of his eyes. "Okay. The short of it is that
my career is on the rocks."

"What's the long of it?"

"The long of it is that I don't know why."

"All right, let me try and get a handle on this," I said.
" 'On the rocks' means you're not getting work?"

"It is very complicated, Jack. It's hints, rumors, feelings
that I get. Plus actual tangible trouble that I'm having with
Warners."

"What kind of trouble?"

"Contract trouble." Adrian put one of those foreign butts
in his mouth and lit up. I offered him a Lucky.

"For the love of God, Walter, those things smell like
yak shit. Take a good old American Lucky."

Adrian smiled and crushed out his cigarette, accepting
one of mine. I lit us both up.

"This contract trouble," the writer continued, plumes
of smoke curling from his nostrils, "is very unusual, Jack.

I've been on the Warners payroll since 1938 and it's the first time we've run into any problem."

"They don't want to renew?"

He shook his head abruptly, either to shut off my line of questioning or to mute the conversation until the waiter, who was setting down our two bowls of barley soup, had departed. When he was out of earshot, Adrian leaned forward and whispered.

"They are giving us money problems."

"And 'us' means you and who else?"

"My agent, Larry Goldmark." Adrian spooned some soup into his mouth, managing to drool a bit on his chin. "The bare facts are this: my current contract runs out on April 6 and we've been renegotiating since December. I was getting twenty-five hundred a week and we asked thirty-five." He looked down into the floating barley, suddenly embarrassed by the gross amounts of money he was talking about.

"Seems fair enough to me," I said. "The way prices are shooting up, how do they expect a fella to live on twenty-five hundred a week?"

Adrian did not find my remark amusing. I had not expected him to.

"Don't bust my nuts, Jack," he said coldly. The writer's moods were as wildly unpredictable as an infant's. "You can't possibly understand the role of money out there."

"I understand the role of money everywhere, Walter. It buys things: slacks, automobiles, legs of lamb, sex, fillets of fish, people."

"No, Jack," he continued, determined to beat his point through my head. "In the movie industry, money is a symbolic gauge of your standing. It measures you and determines your social and professional standing. Exactly and to the dime. Listen, I know the numbers are obscene, wildly out of line. In a world where people live and die in the streets, where children in the capitals of Europe go hungry, where Southern sharecroppers work from dawn to dusk for miserable, grotesque wages, that people should earn a quarter of a million dollars a year to write romance and trash is disgusting. In a decent society, in a society of equals, this wouldn't happen. I know all that, Jack."

Adrian had raised his voice and was punctuating his words by beating his spoon on the table. A platinum blond at the next table and her companion, a fat man with a green cigar in his face, peered at us while pretending to look down at their menus.

"You took the words out of my mouth, Walter," I told him. "Now why don't you slow down and tell me precisely what the problem is. I'll try and keep my bon mots at a minimum."

The writer slumped back in his seat and idly ran his spoon through his soup, making little waves in the bowl.

"You see, Jack," he said in an educational tone, "the studios use dollar amounts to pin labels on people: Big Star, Declining Star, Featured Player. Major Writer, Slipping Writer, Hack. It is very conscious and very, very cruel."

"And you think you're slipping?"

"That's what the negotiations tell me. And I'm baffled, hurt, amazed. I've done great work for Warners in the past couple of years. *Berlin Commando* grossed three million bucks, *Boy From Brooklyn* did two-seven. That's serious dough."

"You don't have to sell me, Walter."

"First, they compromised at three," Adrian went on, picking up speed. "Not what we asked for but good, very good. You never get what you ask for, that's why you ask for it. So they say yes to three and we're about to sign when they come back at us with twenty-five."

Our steaming briskets arrived and the soup bowls were cleared. The waiter wanted to make some bad jokes at our expense by starting a "There's a hundred things on the menu and both these guys order brisket. Where you from,

Cleveland?" spiel. We completely ignored him and he departed in poor humor.

"Same fucking waiters," I muttered.

Walter picked up where he had left off, as if he had been holding his breath. "We were unhappy enough about the twenty-five, but the next day it was down to twenty-two. Like a goddamn stock market crash! I was about to leave for New York and got half-crazy, as you can well imagine. How come I suddenly had the plague? My agent told Warners they could shove the twenty-two. They told him to get wise and accept."

"They give any reasons for this?"

"Reasons?" he bellowed. The platinum lady and the gentleman with the green cigar turned around. Walter blushed and lowered his voice. "Reasons? A collection of excuses, lame excuses, the kind they give when they want you to know they're only lame excuses. They're worried about television, they have to tighten ship, all a lot of crap."

"Walter, this doesn't make too much sense. You're a top screenwriter, a moneymaker. If Warner Brothers is trying to force you down, go somewhere else. You'll find a studio that'll pay you what you want, no?"

Adrian picked at his brisket uneasily.

"I don't think so," he said. "This isn't the time. My agent made some calls: Paramount, Metro, Fox, Selznick. But he couldn't say out front that Warners was trying to cut me out. It was a fishing expedition: he talked vaguely about Walter Adrian wanting to get more freedom. All he got were compliments and the stall."

We ate in silence for a while, Adrian depressed and LeVine hungry. The brisket was lean and aromatic. When we finished, we ordered strawberry cheesecake and coffee, to complete a most excellent glut.

"So where does it stand right now, Walter, as we speak?"

"As we speak?" The writer played with his lip, kneading

15

it between his fingers. "As we speak, it hardly stands at all. The agent told me to sit tight, that if we held out Warners would ultimately give us what we wanted. So I flew East with at least a little peace of mind. Last night I called the Coast." He stared bleakly ahead. "The market has plunged again: they've gone down to seventeen-fifty. And that's just an insult, nothing else."

"If you say so."

Adrian's jaw muscles worked silently and fiercely. "Jack, will you please understand," he said angrily and precisely, "that the dollar amounts are symbolic. The numbers mean they want me out."

"Okay. Now the question is why?"

"I don't have the vaguest."

Our cheesecake was brought forth; gloom and despair briefly vanished. We ate our strawberry-topped wedges with the solemn ecstasy of religious fanatics letting communion wafers dissolve in their mouths. When the last bites began their greased plunges to our respective stomachs, we settled back and called for more coffee. Walter was kind enough to offer me a Havana and I was smart enough to accept. We lit up and sat puffing like a pair of exiled princes. A Negro busboy cleared the dishes.

"Tough job, eh?" Walter asked the busboy in a tone of bogus comradeship.

"Yessir," he replied softly, not looking up from his tray.

"You think seventeen hundred fish per week is a bum salary, kid?" I asked cheerily.

Now he looked up. He was light-skinned and just a boy, eighteen at the most.

"Seventeen hundred?" he asked with a shy smile. "Every week?" He laughed. "No, that's all right with me. You got a job like that?"

"No, but this guy here's got one he wants to give up." I pointed at a fuming Walter.

"Then he's crazy."

"That's what I'm trying to tell him."

The busboy laughed and walked away with his tray full of filthy dishes. Walter was livid, as I knew he would be.

"What the hell was that all about?" he demanded. "I didn't know you enjoyed humiliating your friends."

"I'll tell you what it is, Walter. I hammer at weak spots. By now it's an instinct. See, the thing is, I don't think you're leveling with me. You came into my office to feel me out and told me someone was tailing you. That was the bunk, but I can understand why you did it. But now you allegedly feel comfortable with me and you're still not leveling. That's what I don't like."

"I *am* leveling, Jack."

"You aren't. I can't believe that you don't have a single clue as to why Warner Brothers is out to get you. What is it, Walter, a morals rap? They catch you sashaying around in one of Virginia Mayo's outfits? You shtup someone you're not supposed to, like Warner's daughter or Minnie Mouse or The Three Stooges? What is it? A clue, a hint is all I want. Even if you're not sure, give me your suspicions."

Walter shook his head in helplessness, not so much at my questions, but at his situation.

"It is not morals, Jack. I'm absolutely sure about that."

"And it's obviously not incompetence, not if your pictures have been making dough."

"A high percentage have been profitable, Jack. You can look it up in *Variety*."

"Oh, I believe it, Walter," I told him. "Doesn't leave much, except studio politics, personal animus."

The writer nodded vaguely. "I have some enemies there," he said slowly, as if diagraming his thoughts, "but don't we all? Hollywood has cliques like any place else, probably more because it's such an insular community. There are the old-timers, the old money, the progressive element. . . ." His voice trailed off, his eyes got distant and unfocused.

"It is politics, then," I said quietly.

Adrian looked at me and I could tell for sure that he was trying to decide how far he could go with me.

"In a general sense you might be right, Jack." He weighed the words out, gram by gram. The calibrations were minute. "There are rumors that it might be a bad time for people like us."

"Who's 'us,' Jews?"

"People with progressive ideas. People who care a little about the world, about the sufferings of humanity, about the direction of government." The writer's eyes caught fire. "Christ, Jack, don't you remember back in '27, at City, when the Sacco–Vanzetti case blew up, the anguish of our generation? It was all we could think about, it was a watershed, a dividing line. What did Dos Passos write? 'All right we are two nations.' It was such a revelation." Adrian leaned across the table, his face inches from mine. "We had such ideas about the way the world was going to be, Jack! God, did we ever dream! We were fools in college, of course; our ideas were unformed, undisciplined, but our instincts were right. I still make mistakes, I spread myself too thin, but I keep trying." He shook his head thoughtfully. "Trouble is, there's so much to learn about and the world changes so quickly you can't truly keep abreast of things. But that can't stop us from caring deeply or thinking deeply about the forces that make governments tick. Particularly with these terrible weapons of war we have now. One wrong move and it's all up in smoke. And the United States won't share the secret. That's why, now more than ever, the people who want a better world can't be scared off."

Adrian's eyes had grown bright and intense, thrilled by his own oratory. I cleared my throat.

"Stop me if I'm wrong," I began, "but are you telling me that you spoke out too often and you're getting roasted for it?"

"I wish to God I knew."

"Okay. Anything else to tell me?"

"There's nothing else to tell."

"You ever do any work for Uncle Joe Stalin? Used to be very, very popular, Walter. Lot of smart people did."

Adrian leaned so far forward in his chair that he was practically out of it.

"I've only worked for the people of the world," he said. "Believe me, Jack."

Which was all I needed to hear. The part of my brain that I like the best told me to get Adrian out of my life pronto. He was hazy, evasive, and trouble all around. But he was so obviously scared and such a pigeon for anybody with an angle that I knew I had to climb in the boat with him, leaky as it might be. I had the feeling he was going to need a lot of help, the kind of help he wouldn't get from his agents and managers. Besides, I told myself, it had been a dull few months: follow this guy, follow that broad, hang around that lobby. What for, to make a buck? Any shoe salesman can make a buck. LeVine rationalizes.

"Are you asking me to go to the Coast, Walter?"

He nodded. "Exactly. I want you to find out the precise reasons and motives behind all this trouble. I don't know much, Jack, but I know this is serious."

"And you're not being cute with me—you really don't know why you're being pushed around?"

He covered my hand with his.

"Trust me, shamus."

So I trusted him and if that doesn't keep LeVine out of the private dicks' hall of fame, nothing ever will. Adrian agreed to fly me out to the Coast and pay me three hundred dollars plus expenses for a ten-day investigation, to begin the following Wednesday, one week hence. He wrote a check covering the air fare.

"I'll get you a room at the Camino Real and have a car waiting for you there. Take a cab from the airport."

"Fine." I folded the check and put it in my wallet.

Adrian nodded and sat a little awkwardly, his hands bunched in his lap.

75132

"I've never hired a detective before." He flashed his best boyish smile.

"You'll get used to it," I told him. "It's like hiring any menial help."

He nodded some more and then, having nothing further to say to each other, we got up and paid the tab.

Out on the street, crowds of people streamed toward their eight-thirty curtains. Adrian and I stood with our hands in our pockets.

"You're going home now, Jack?"

"Yeah. I walk down to Times Square and catch the Flushing train."

"Trains run pretty regularly?"

"The Flushing is pretty good."

Adrian removed his hand from his pocket and extended it for a final shake. I shook it.

"Then I'll see you a week from tonight in California. We'll treat you like a king." Adrian was attempting to infuse the mission with a little gaiety, but he was too burdened by fears and doubts to come very close.

"I'll be there, Walter."

"Wonderful. I'll be flying out tomorrow." He tightened his grip on my hand. "And thanks for helping me out, Jack. I think you know how much it means to me."

"Don't thank me, I'm being well paid for this job."

"I know you're not doing it for the money."

I wasn't sure if he was right, so I kept my silence. We stood uneasily on the street, reluctant to part company but uncomfortable in each other's presence. I finally made the move.

"Take it easy, Walter. I'm sure we'll work this out for the best."

He slapped me on the shoulder and I headed south on Broadway. One block later, I stopped at a light and turned around. Walter Adrian was still in front of Lindy's, tall and well dressed and alone.

2

I don't like airplanes, being a person apt to worry even when both my Florsheims are planted firmly on the earth, so you can imagine what the thirteen-hour flight to Los Angeles did for my disposition. The DC-6 was jammed to capacity and there wasn't enough room between the seats to cross a pair of adult male legs, so I spent a good deal of the trip pacing the aisles like an expectant father. My attempts at flirtation with the stewardesses were brushed off with professional ease, and a blond I had a casual eye on spent the last half of the trip straddling the armrest of a boisterous and wavy-haired Boston advertising man. She giggled and mussed his hair; he whispered in her ear and she took on the moist and serene look of someone whose glands have just said·yes. The spectacle made me very unhappy, less for romantic reasons than for the fact that fantasizing about the blond had been a way of passing time. That fantasy shut off, I was condemned to spend the rest of the journey reading newspapers and worrying about Walter Adrian.

After stops in Washington and Dallas, we set down for good at a quarter past five in the afternoon. I exited the plane on legs of stone and crossed the damp and breezy airstrip at an arthritic pace. The baggage pickup was a quarter-mile away, a trek across wooden walkways that bisected construction sites of mud and timber. The L.A. airport was a jerry-built affair of squat buildings in varying states of renovation and disembowelment. Palm trees swayed in the warm wet air and it was no trick to imagine one's arrival in a banana republic whose aerodrome was being rebuilt as a monument to some national hero with a thin mustache and a Swiss bank account.

My Central American fantasy was not discouraged by the sloth of the baggage handling. I waited for a half hour in the stifling American Airlines shed while stray pieces of luggage came sliding down a metal chute, one by one. I noticed that the blond had gotten pretty drunk and was leaning heavily on the arm of the Boston ad man, who had the unhappy appearance of one whose plans for the evening were souring and out of control.

When the leather suitcase with the gold "J. LeV." came down the chute, I grabbed it before the redcaps could and hustled outside to hail a cab. It was already six o'clock and I wanted to see Adrian before the transcontinental lag in time made me too sleepy to think straight.

A row of hacks was waiting outside the baggage shed. The first in line, a chunky, impassive Mexican with a deep scar on his forehead, signaled to me and took my bag. I said "Camino Real" and he nodded solemnly, placing my suitcase in the trunk with the gentle care of a man returning his infant daughter to her bed. He held the back door for me and I got into the cab. This was nothing, nothing at all, like New York. The hackie did not speak as he pulled out into traffic, not about the weather or politics or the Dodgers. I was in a foreign land.

That sense of foreignness accelerated as I settled in for the ride to the hotel. Palms stood full and gawky before a sky turning from pale secret blue to gaudy Hollywood sunset pink. White and salmon stucco houses, their roofs spiny red tile, glowed with a kind of doomsday phosphorescence. Windows burned off reflected pinks and oranges; behind them I supposed wives were preparing suppers for husbands but it was hard to imagine. No people sat in yards or took down wash; perhaps only fruit baskets occupied these jukebox-colored houses. I lowered my chin into a moist palm and felt that mixture of bemusement and sick-to-the-gut loneliness that comes with entering a strange city. And there is, I learned, no city stranger than Los Angeles, even to its inhabitants.

My sense of time and place was bent completely out of whack. It was that most numbing and private hour, sunset, and I stared out the windows of this cab wondering what the hell I was doing in California, so far from my small comforts. The more I speculated on the Adrian tale, the more half-baked the whole venture seemed, three hundred bills or not. I knew nothing about the writer's life or the worlds in which he moved, nothing about his friends or enemies. I didn't know the good guys from the heavies, the golden girls from the floozies. I wasn't even sure I could really trust Adrian; God knows what he might have flown me out here for. To be his alibi, to save his marriage. People with money can exercise their whims in a more dramatic fashion than can those without it.

I massaged my brain in this useless fashion all the way to the hotel, located on a residential Hollywood street called Sierra Bonita, just off Sunset Boulevard. The Camino Real was three stories of unpretentious white stucco separated from the street by a driveway which curved around a broad lawn boasting a slightly oily lily pond. I paid the Mexican, somnambulated through the Spanish-style lobby of wrought iron railings and red tile floors, and was led to my room by an elderly priss named Roy. He told me I looked like the rugged type. I congratulated him on his perception and closed the door in his face.

Adrian had gotten me a large and airy back room. It overlooked a small patio set in a grove of fragrant fruit trees, but I was too tired to enjoy it. I flopped down on the soft double bed and closed my eyes. It was a quarter to seven. What I really wanted to do was grab some dinner, go to sleep, and check in with Adrian early the next morning. But I rarely do what I want to do, who of us does? So I sat up and decided to get right on the case.

Funny thing is the case was practically over.

When I called Adrian's house a woman answered. I asked if she was Helen Adrian. She sounded guarded.

"Yes, this is. Who am I speaking to?"

"It's Jack LeVine, Mrs. Adrian, from New York."

"Walter's friend the private eye?" She sounded relieved.

"Himself. In person."

"Well, it's just marvelous that you're here. Walter's been raving about you." Helen Adrian had the kind of husky and unvarnished voice that usually went with women I got silly over.

"Walter always raves. Can I speak to him?"

"Well, Jack, Walter's still at the studio. He's working late on a rewrite that was due five days ago."

"So he's still working?"

"Oh yes. Contract squabbles or not. He's devoted to his work." I couldn't separate the irony from the admiration. Both were present in her voice.

"How's he been?"

"Up and down," she said carefully. "Mainly down. As far as I know, his agent and Warners are still negotiating. Apparently they're starting to give in a little and Larry—that's Larry Goldmark, Walter's agent—thinks there might have been some misunderstanding all along. But he's not sure."

"Sounds vague as hell."

"Doesn't it? This business really stinks, Jack, you can't imagine." Her words were bitter but the tone remained detached, analytical.

"I'll have to learn," I told her. "Listen, will I be able to see Walter tonight?" I hoped she'd say no.

"Of course," she said. "He left a gate pass for you at the studio, so there won't be any trouble getting in. And we dropped the car off at the Real last night. It's in the garage. You know how to get to Warners?"

I told her no and she gave me the directions, which were relatively uncomplicated. Sunset to Highland to Cahuenga Boulevard through something called the Cahuenga Pass; from there to Barham Boulevard, which led directly to a complex of hangar-like sound stages, which was Warner Brothers.

"Then I'll get off the phone and go see him, Mrs. Adrian."

"Wonderful." Her voice went cautious again. "Watch out for him, Jack. This is a terrible time for Walter."

I told her that I knew it, then hung up. I left the room, locked up and immediately unlocked and returned to the room. I took my gun out of the suitcase and slipped it into my jacket pocket. Then I left again, for real.

I took the elevator down to the hotel garage and found my car, a black 1947 Chrysler New Yorker, not quite as long as an aircraft carrier but every bit as practical. The interior was plushly customized, with ripe tomato red upholstery and a highly polished wooden dashboard containing so many dials and gauges that I couldn't decide whether to drive the car or fly it. When I opened the glove compartment to find some kind of owner's manual, all I discovered was a box of Kleenex and a note from Adrian: "Dear Jack —Welcome to Hollywood! Hope the car is to your liking. Best, Walter." The car was not to my liking. I started the engine and shifted into reverse, at which point the front end started clattering like two milk bottles rolling down a flight of stairs, until the engine died. I performed this comic pantomime two more times, to the kittenish amusement of

25

a long-legged young woman, who waved at me and pulled out of the garage in a red Buick convertible, hitting fifty as she went up the ramp. I tried starting in gear. The car lurched forward. I stepped on the brake and practically sailed out the windshield, at which point it dawned on me that the car had an automatic transmission and that the clutch was as functionless as a wax banana. You could shift, if you were so inclined, but only from second to third. LeVine victimized by somebody's idea of progress.

Driving as gingerly as a man astride a pair of horses, I maneuvered the Chrysler into evening traffic, easily finding my way to Highland and Cahuenga. It was getting quite dark, but a last thin slice of western sky glowed the smoky electric yellow of a radio dial. Speeding along Cahuenga, everything broke down into points of light: headlights, taillights, and the blinking, star-like lights of the tract homes spread like crushed ice across the valley floors. You could see for many miles ahead. I sat back in my seat, steering with one hand and gazing out at the plowed fields of light. Again, the foreigner.

I got off Cahuenga at Barham and took a right. After three or four miles, I reached the top of a rise and saw the grayish sound stages of Warner Brothers crouched in the distance like a herd of elephants asleep in the brush. Lights were on, but the studio parking lots were nearly empty. It was an undeniable gee-whiz kick seeing the back lot for the first time, and I slowed down to let it sink in. There lay the place where Rita Hayworth got undressed, the back alleys where Cagney and Bogart slapped guys around. Someone started honking in back of me and I accelerated, down the hill to the dreamworks.

There was a main gate, and a center island with a small office staffed by a couple of guys wearing studio blazers. One of them stopped me as I drove in.

"Evening, sir," he said brightly. "Name please?"

"Jack LeVine."

He lowered his young blond head and leafed through some orange slips of paper attached to a clipboard he was holding.

"L–e capital v–i–n–e?"

"Correct. Walter Adrian left me a pass."

He inserted one of the orange slips under the windshield wiper.

"All right, Mr. LeVine," he said. "You will find Mr. Adrian in the Writer's Building. Just go straight up, take your second left and then another and you'll double back to the Writer's Building. It is roughly parallel to where we are right now."

"How late do you folks stay open?" I asked.

He grinned. "Always and forever. That's what movies are all about." He pointed. "That's two lefts."

I followed his directions and arrived in a small parking lot occupied by perhaps a half-dozen cars, very large and elaborate cars. The lot was adjacent to a three-story white building, inevitably stucco and red-roofed. This was the un-imposing lair of Warners' writers. The modesty of the building was a blind; inside, there were guys typing in cubby-holes who pulled down five grand each and every week. A lot of them had gone home; half the windows in the place were dark. On the bottom floor I could see a couple of men arguing in a medium-sized office. They were drinking highballs and making a lot of sweeping hand gestures; the younger of the two men was pacing back and forth. It appeared to be a friendly argument. Finally, the older guy, a bald man in horn-rimmed glasses and a v-neck sweater that revealed a patch of graying chest hair, broke into peals of unfelt laughter. He arose from his chair and slapped the younger man on the back, then led him out of the office with his arm draped around his shoulder. Without know-ing the particulars, I was pretty sure that the younger man was getting the raw end of it.

I walked inside and headed down a long corridor lined with offices on both sides. Each door was marked with a shingle bearing someone's name. I didn't recognize the names. A woman in her forties was locking up an office at the far end. She observed me wandering aimlessly about.

"May I help you?" she asked.

"I'm looking for Walter Adrian's office."

She pointed to a set of double doors.

"He's upstairs."

He wasn't upstairs. When I got to Adrian's office, the door was open and the lights were on, but the chair behind the desk was empty. There was a piece of paper on the floor. I picked it up and saw that my name was on it. "Jack—Am on the Western Street at far tip of back lot. Blocking out some action for overdue rewrite. Meet me there. Best, Walter." It must have blown on the floor. I dropped the note in my pocket and left Adrian's office in a foul temper. I had been running ever since disembarking from the plane, and every time I got someplace it turned out to be nowhere at all.

I was further delighted to learn that I was nearly a half-mile from the Western Street. A maintenance man directed me to follow the main center strip of Warners down to the end, and then hang every conceivable right.

The back lot began at the terminus of the main studio drag. It was quite a show. At seven-thirty on a warm Wednesday night in Southern California, I stood in a replica of my childhood, surrounded by the tenements and store fronts of the Lower East Side. It was fraud, deceit, and gross tampering with my emotions. As anxious as I was to see Adrian, I walked very slowly down this street, savoring the Hebrew signs, the Italian grocery stores and bakeries, the stoops and iron railings and chalk-scrawled pavements. It was as empty as a midnight graveyard on what a signpost said was Hester Street. My old sweet Hester Street, lovingly duplicated but chillingly unpopulated. It was post-atomic war Hester Street. I stood at a dead lamppost and lit a cigarette and, yes, I felt like George Raft. With a hitch of my shoulders, I continued on down the street, my shoes thunderous on the pavement. I anticipated the razzing of the Dead End Kids, or a tip of the cap from patrolman Ward Bond, and I wished—as I have always wished—that Ann Sheridan would emerge from a doorway, take one look at me, and realize that here was the man she had been waiting for.

There was a green newsstand at the corner, shuttered and peeling. When I passed it, I left the Lower East Side and entered Prohibition Chicago. Black sedans were parked at the curb and yellow election posters were placed in the smoked windows of O'Casey's Bar. The Gem Cinema was across the street, but the lights were off and the marquee was blank. The buildings and cars had been used much too often; they appeared to be in bad need of repair, but the magic still worked. I knew this place with the certainty of dream-knowledge; a dozen movies had burned every cornice and bit of masonry into my brain cells. This was the street of swells in tuxedos, of platinum blonds, of gunmen rolling in the gutters. I stood with my hands in my pockets, awed and self-conscious, knowing I didn't belong here.

Past the sidewalk cafés and dress shops of Paris, the plaza and bleached walls of a Mexican village, ten yards of downtown Berlin, and into Anyville, U.S.A., identifiable by white picket fences, home sweet homes, and Junior's jalopy parked out front. It was goyische heaven, as foreign to me as the Casbah, which was right around the corner, a cheat of whitewashed walls and tacky vendors' stalls. A cobbled alleyway led me out.

And directly into the Western Street.

It was the largest area on the whole back lot, a complete frontier town built around a wide dirt street that took a dogleg curve to the right. The street was lined with buildings, real and fake-front, on both sides, but it was too dark to make them out very clearly. It was very quiet, except for the high and low notes of a wind that blew with unobstructed force down the wide and dusty street. Something toppled over in the distance, something small but heavy,

29

like a cart or wheelbarrow. I strained to see Walter walking about, but couldn't, so I called his name. The wind blew the words back in my face and I received no reply.

I started up the street, past a hotel, livery stable, blacksmith, and notions shop to my right; to the left lay the inevitable saloon, dry goods store, and a jailhouse with barred front windows and a gallows complete with dangling dummy in the back. I went over to the saloon and pushed through the swinging doors. Inside was a wooden bar, all right, but the rest of the room was a technicians' chaos of wood shavings, pieces of cable, a large arc light laid on its side, and a muddy porridge of rags and rope and pages of script gathered in a janitor's careful pile in the corner. The wind blew the doors back and forth, and I backed out of the room in a gunfighter's crouch, hands at the ready.

Back on the street, I again called for Walter and drew another blank. I walked around the dogleg bend, past the church, schoolhouse, and large red barn. I tried the barn, tugging hard at a tall jammed door. It screeched open on unoiled hinges. There was no light inside. I cupped my hand around a match and saw more electronic litter strewn about. I walked out, leaving the door open, and traced my steps back down the street, intending to return to the Writer's Building. I strode past the dry goods store and the jailhouse. The gallows creaked in the wind and the lonely dummy swung to and fro. I stopped in my tracks and stared. A queasy, icy sweat drenched my entire body.

It was not a dummy.

It was Walter Adrian.

Adrian's dead eyes looked merely surprised. His tongue was protruding and I wanted to put it back where it belonged, but I knew I couldn't tamper with what was now one hundred and sixty pounds of evidence. Evidence of what, I did not know. I just kind of held Walter, as if to stop the strangling, then figured what the hell, and let go. He swung back and forth, slowly, heavily, and the wooden planks groaned in the evening silence. I'd run into enough stiffs in my time, but this one really hurt bad. I wanted to cut him down, to help him some, because that's what he had flown me out here for, to help him, but rearranging a body, any body, is not a clever thing to do.

So LeVine stood there and tried to catch his breath, in back of the jailhouse at Warner Brothers. When I had my breath and a few of my wits back, I felt around Walter's clothing for a note of some kind, coming up empty except for a scrap of notebook paper with scribbling on it: "Check pos. stables. Jailhouse?" I decided to put the note in my pocket, then climbed the gallows steps. There was nothing much up there, again no suicide note. I noticed a little blood on the edge of the opening through which Adrian had fallen, blood smeared thin and already drying. I knelt down and felt the back of Walter's head. There was a partial swelling. It figured that he'd cracked his head going down. On the assumption it was suicide, an assumption I was in no big hurry to accept.

I looked down at my old cafeteria chum gone Hollywood and the questions started percolating. Why would he conceivably finish himself off? Why back here? Why summon me out West, if only to croak himself on the day of my anticipated arrival? The questions found nothing resembling answers. All I could think about was how lousy I felt. I climbed down the wooden steps, took a last look at Walter Adrian and said good-bye to him. I might even have squeezed his hand. Then I started back to the Writer's Building. The wind was blowing harder now and it was time to call the cops.

lieutenant named Wynn was running the show. He was sitting in Adrian's chair behind Adrian's desk, smoking a Stummel pipe and trying to come up with a plausible, i.e., suspicious, reason for me to have been looking for the screenwriter on the Western Street at Warners in the dark.

"Okay, let's take it from the top," he said for the third time. "You came in from New York today, via an airplane."

"Via an airplane is correct."

"Why?"

"Because the stagecoach don't run no more."

"You're killing me," he said evenly. "I'll rephrase the question: why did you come out here?"

"Like I said five minutes ago, I'm an old friend of Walter's."

"An old friend who just happens to be a peeper." Wynn pretended to laugh and played with the keys of Adrian's typewriter. He was a small wiry man, with pitted olive-yellow skin and gray-green eyes that were at once bored and unhappy. You could have lost a small dog in his eyebrows; the cop's hairline appeared to begin at the bridge of his nose. Wynn's teeth were stained horse-yellow from his pipe sucking, and his lips were as thin as two blades of grass. He was professionally hostile, but not ugly hostile; just unimaginative, dull, and a pain in the neck.

Wynn had two other detectives along for the ride and they sat with exaggerated disinterest in two canvas chairs against the wall. They were called Lemon and Caputo and they were as sharp as a couple of bowling balls. Lemon had dirty blond hair and the sullen pudginess of a beach boy gone to fat; Caputo was tall, dark, and wide. He kept a small smile and a large hat on the entire time.

"Even peepers have friends, Lieutenant," I told Wynn.

"Not the ones I know." He aimed bluish smoke at the ceiling.

"He was dead when you got there?" asked Lemon. It was his first question, but Wynn had already asked the same one twice.

"Not quite. He was finishing an aria from 'Pagliacci.' Then he died."

"Your good friend croaks and you make funnies," Wynn mumbled in fake solemnity. "I don't figure it."

"Listen, he was a friend, but not my closest buddy on earth," I told him. "Who are we kidding? I ran into him in New York and he asked me to come out here and check on something for him. I got here, went directly to the studio, and found him dead. I am stunned, upset, and confused. But he was not, repeat not, my very best friend."

"And you don't know what the trouble was?" Wynn asked.

"No."

"And you flew out here anyways?" This was Caputo's contribution. He looked at Wynn as he said it, but Wynn was looking at his pipe.

"For three hundred bucks, I'll fly to a lot of places," I told Caputo. "Also, like I said, he was a friend."

"But not a good friend," Wynn said softly.

"That's right."

Wynn put his hands on Adrian's desk and hoisted himself up. Caputo and Lemon rose from their seats like twin slices of toast.

"I guess that'll be it for now, Levine," the lieutenant said.

"LeVine, like Hollywood and Vine."

"I don't care how you pronounce it. In my book L–e–v–i–n–e is Levine."

"Except in my case."

"Fuck it. LeVine." He didn't have the energy to squabble over the matter. "Anyhow, don't fly out of town or we'll fly you back at your expense. I'm pretty sure this is suicide and I'd like to wrap it up by tomorrow or the next." He paused and donned his hat. "But I don't like that he needed a peeper."

"He didn't like it either," I told Wynn.

"I'll bet he didn't." The cop shook his head in a lawman's bewilderment at the endless variety of human folly. "What'd a guy like that make, couple g's a week?"

"Something like that," I said.

"So he strings himself up." It was beyond him, beyond me as well. Wynn stared at me carefully. "He queer?"

"Not that I know of. I hadn't seen him for a long time before New York, but I never knew him to go that way."

"People change out here," the lieutenant said. "It's the sun does it. They want to try everything."

"I'd be surprised, Lieutenant, that's all I'm saying."

"Okay." Wynn turned to the court jesters. "Let's beat it."

"You know," I told Wynn, "if it's not suicide, it's murder."

He didn't bat an eye. "Not if I can help it. There's no evidence of homicide. And thank God for it. Movie industry murders are nothing but trouble. Let's clean this up fast and neat, huh, LeVine? Seems to me there's been enough pain here already."

He turned and walked out of the office, trailed by Huey and Looey. Wynn was a lot brighter than I first guessed, and instinct told him to close the case. I sat behind Walter

Adrian's desk for a few silent minutes, waiting to hear what my instincts had to say.

They finally spoke up, and then I left the Writer's Building for an apprehensive ride to the home of Walter's new widow.

The Adrian house was located in the Sherman Oaks section of Los Angeles, a couple of miles northwest of Hollywood. I rehearsed my heartbreaking revelation all the way over, until it sounded so polished and elegant as to be altogether useless. If your husband just died at the end of a rope, dangling in the wind like a side of beef, carefully chosen words could not cover the ugliness any more than a new suit could make him look alive. I decided to drop the frills and pauses and tell it straight.

My decision was beside the point. By the time I arrived at the huge Tudor-style home on Escadero Road, the driveway was already crowded with cars, one of which belonged to the Los Angeles Police Department. The news had been broken, the news had spread.

I parked across the street and walked over to the sprawling, elegant, two-story house. It looked like a refugee from some sheltered, old-money eastern neighborhood, the kind with its own security force. A double chimney blew white smoke into the night air, huge sheltering trees brushed their limbs against the roof. All the lights were on and I didn't want to be there.

As I walked up the front steps, two cops emerged from a side door and got into their squad car. The car backed slowly out of the driveway, its red light flashing in a gesture that seemed more ceremonial than official. It went up the street, turned right, and vanished.

I rang the bell. It chimed loudly, over the mortuary-pitched conversation of what sounded like close to a dozen people gathered inside. A pale, stocky man with a bulbous nose and curly hair came to the door and stared at me. He was wearing glasses with lenses so thick that his eyes seemed to float hugely behind them, like dark stones on the floor of a fish tank.

"Yes?"

"My name is Jack LeVine, a friend . . ."

"Of course," the man said softly, opening the door and stepping to one side, "the private detective who found Walter." He held out his hand as I entered. "I am Milton Wohl, a screenwriter and a dear friend of Walter's."

I shook Milton Wohl's small, damp hand—imagine squeezing a pork kidney—and stepped into a foyer. The house was dense with hushed and urgent conversation, rich with the odors of liquor and perfume.

"Do you know Helen?" Wohl asked solicitously.

"No, I don't."

"Fine," he said, for no reason at all. The writer was clearly shaken by the events of the evening. "I'll introduce you."

Wohl led me into the living room and I got an inkling of the kind of life Walter had lived in Hollywood. The room was at least forty feet long, with polished wooden beams lining the low ceiling. A fireplace took up the far wall, flanked on either side by full suits of armor blindly guarding the blaze, the iron plate glowing a dull, Dark Ages orange. Bookshelves lined the paneled walls, jammed to overflowing with leather-bound classics and popular fiction, pre-Columbian figurines, and somebody's favorite collection of little glass elephants.

Small spotlights were affixed to the ceiling, shining on a series of brilliant medieval illuminations depicting the progress of an autumnal battle for someone's honor. Horses reared, their curiously human eyes staring at the heavens, bearing faceless warriors on their backs. A golden-haired woman, clutching a red arrow and a torch, hovered in the air. She looked bemused.

The woman on the couch by the fireplace was neither golden-haired nor bemused. Her hair was long and red, and she was as beautiful as any woman I have ever seen. She rose and walked toward me.

"Helen," said Wohl, "this is Jack LeVine."

"I am so terribly sorry," I told her.

Unexpectedly, and to the evident surprise and faint displeasure of the men and women standing and sitting about the room, Helen Adrian embraced me. I tentatively hugged her in return. She looked up at me, her jade-green eyes touched with red.

"It must have been horrible for you, Jack."

"Pretty rough."

"You'll have a drink?"

"Please. Bourbon and water."

"Of course." She turned to Wohl. "Milt, could you get Jack a bourbon and water?"

Wohl examined me curiously, his eyes submerged in still water behind the bullet-proof specs. Then he slipped away, less than delighted to be handling the butler duties.

"Sit beside me, Jack," said Mrs. Adrian, lightly touching my lapel. "Let's talk for a while."

She led me across the room, all eyes following our progress. I felt like the proverbial bare-assed gentleman in Macy's window. We sat down on a long yellow couch, directly in front of the fire. Mrs. Adrian moved close to me and all I could do was stare. It was not any particular feature that so astonished me, not the delicately arched nose or the perfect teeth or the remarkably large and attentive eyes; it was, rather, a white hot intelligence that gave her face its poised and startling symmetry. I couldn't get over her. She was most certainly in shock, but it seemed to me a surface condition. Dive below to the heart, or up to the brain, and you would find someone with a firm hold on reality.

She leaned very close to me. "Jack, the police said it was suicide," she whispered. "I don't believe that."

"Why not?"

"He's been upset, but not that upset. It's not in Walter's character to do that. He's not a quitter." She spoke precisely, emphatically.

"No, he wasn't." I made the painful change in tense. I didn't really know whether Adrian was a quitter or not. At this point, it hardly seemed to matter. "But he was very much in the dumps when we spoke in New York."

Mrs. Adrian reached over and picked a large brandy snifter off an end table. A couple of shots of cognac glittered in the lamp and firelight; she swirled the liquid about and gazed down into the glass, a fawn at a pond. There was a tap on my shoulder. Wohl with my drink. I took it and thanked him. He looked fondly at Mrs. Adrian.

"She's taking it marvelously, isn't she?" said the writer, as if she wasn't there. "Just marvelously."

Mrs. Adrian looked up at him. "You don't have to stay here, Milton, really." She smiled, just a little. "Please don't feel that you have to."

Wohl didn't know if he was being paid a compliment or asked to leave. The fire behind us lit his thick glasses into two miniature blazes. He nodded and sipped some ginger ale.

"Milton was Walter's best friend," said Mrs. Adrian. "He's been so terribly wounded by this." Now it was like Wohl wasn't there.

The writer leaned over and whispered in my ear. "I'd like a few words with you when you're done with Helen," he said, then straightened himself and joined a few other people who were standing in a clump, intently watching Helen and me talk.

"He really Walter's best pal or was that just talk?" I asked Mrs. Adrian.

"Everyone was Walter's best pal. That was his problem." Her voice turned a little bitter.

"This would seem to be the wrong town for deep friendships."

"God, is it ever." She downed some cognac. "I mean,

38

Walter could be as calculating as everyone else out here. It's a law of nature. But down deep he was so goddamn trusting." Her face crumpled up, then she turned her head and abruptly wept into a corner of the couch. It was way overdue. I patted her on the shoulder.

"Why don't you go stretch out for a while," I told her. "Cry your eyes out. It's time to stop being brave."

A thick-featured and large-boned woman in a peasant blouse and blue skirt appeared. Her hair was wrapped in a bun so tight it looked to be pulling her face in half.

"Helen, take Mr. LeVine's advice," she said not too gently. "You ought to get some rest."

Mrs. Adrian got up slowly. She sighed, and looked to be ready for a long cry.

"Jack LeVine, this is Rachel Wohl, Milton's wife." She made a last attempt at playing hostess. "You'll come back here tomorrow, Jack, around suppertime?"

"Of course," I told her, aware that everyone had heard the invitation.

Mrs. Adrian took my hand and squeezed it as hard as she could, which wasn't very hard at all. Then she circled the room and thanked everyone before heading up the stairs, followed by Rachel Wohl. When she disappeared from view, the volume in the room went up a decibel or two, as if a cautious hand had adjusted a knob.

I stood up and Wohl sprang to my side.

"You're not leaving, are you?" he asked.

"Thought I'd circulate."

Wohl smiled agreeably and took my arm. "Fine. You must meet some of us."

The writer shepherded me over to a tense group of people seated in a semicircle by the bar. They included the sandy-haired cowboy actor Dale Carpenter, screenwriter Carroll Arthur, Jr., and his wife June, Henry Perillo, a carpenter and an official in the International Alliance of Theatrical Stage Employees, a German composer of movie scores named Sig Friedland, and Adrian's agent, Larry

Goldmark. I was greeted with the restrained enthusiasm usually accorded an insurance salesman.

"Pull up a seat," said Goldmark, a pale, svelte figure of perhaps forty. He was drinking and chewing gum at the same time.

Wohl got a chair for me. "We want to hear all about it, Jack. And don't think you have to spare us; we'd like to know exactly what happened."

"So would I," I told him. Wohl got himself a hassock and we both sat down. "What do you want to hear about, folks?"

Goldmark looked at the others, knotting his hands together. "Did he leave any kind of a note?" he asked.

"Why in the back lot, for heaven's sake?" blurted Carroll Arthur, Jr. Arthur had pasty cratered skin and was quite drunk. I don't think he heard Goldmark's question. "Why the back lot?"

"I don't know why the back lot," I said. "No worse a place than any. If you don't die in your own bed, you might as well croak in a Ferris wheel. That's my opinion."

"The note?" asked Dale Carpenter, clearly troubled behind his blankly handsome features.

"Yes, LeVine, a note?" This was Perillo, a stocky man with broad shoulders, a crewcut, and an earnest, friendly manner. His brown eyes protruded a bit, like Peter Lorre's.

Rachel Wohl came down the stairs.

"How's she doing?" I asked.

"She's strong as an ox," Mrs. Wohl answered, with some admiration but very little love. She took a seat and peered at me coldly. "I hear talk about a note. What did it say? Did it mention anyone?"

Wohl threw his wife a murderous glance and she reddened.

"Did it give a reason?" she forged on, then turned on her husband. "For Christ's sake, Milt, stop staring at me! I know what I'm doing!" June Arthur started sniffling into her handkerchief. This was a very relaxed group of people.

"Folks, it is no business of mine to say whether or not Walter left a note," I said, "let alone give it a dramatic reading."

"Why?" demanded Mrs. Wohl.

"Because notes are much too private. It's Mrs. Adrian's prerogative," I told her.

"He's right," said Perillo.

"Thank you." We smiled at each other, like two attendants in a lunatic asylum.

"I agree," said Friedland. That made three.

"Did you read the note, LeVine?" asked Carpenter.

"I didn't say there was a note. I'm saying that if there was, it's up to Helen Adrian to do with it what she wants. Now if there *wasn't* a note, maybe it wasn't suicide." I looked around and sipped my bourbon. "Anybody here know why someone would want to spring a trapdoor under Walter?"

I was always a terrible party pooper. There weren't any gasps, that's only in the Charlie Chan movies, but it got as quiet as a serious game of poker. Noses were rubbed, feet and hands were contemplated. The composer Friedland, a heavy-set man with red cheeks, untamed curls, and steel-rimmed spectacles, finally cleared his throat. In the silence, it registered like the downshifting of a truck.

"You are suggesting a murder, perhaps, Mr. LeVine?" was his thoughtful, heavily-accented question.

"I'm suggesting it, but not claiming it. I don't have any special information, Mr. Friedland. All I found was a dead man."

"Then there *wasn't* a note." Carpenter jumped on my words like a lawyer.

"Jesus Christ," I muttered. "Murder doesn't exclude a faked note, typed up and inserted in the victim's pocket. But why won't anyone tell me whether Walter had the kind of enemies who might conceivably do him in?"

"He didn't have those kind of enemies," said Goldmark. "People in the industry loved Walter."

41

"And Walter loved Walter, too," mumbled Arthur. "It's all nuts."

"I'm with Arthur," I said. "So far, nothing matches."

"Walter was very despondent recently," said Perillo. "Terribly so. Why do you doubt suicide, Mr. LeVine?"

"It's my job to doubt things. That's why Walter hired me. But let me accept suicide. Okay, now why are you all so scared of a note? What do you think Walter wrote on it?"

The sound got shut off again. Goldmark got up and walked to a corner of the living room; with a twitch of his eyebrows, he gestured for me to join him. As I did, Wohl huddled with Carpenter, Perillo, and Carroll Arthur. Arthur had trouble getting to his feet.

Goldmark was chewing gum furiously. He winked at me. "You struck a nerve, LeVine," he said quietly, lighting an Old Gold and squinting as the smoke sailed directly into his eyes.

"What goes on? I walk into a wake and it turns into Twenty Questions."

"Things are happening," Goldmark said.

"Thanks for the tip. Can I see you tomorrow?"

Goldmark looked over his shoulder, back to where Adrian's friends were buzzing among themselves.

"Why?"

"I'd like to know what happened to Walter."

"He died. Let it be, LeVine. Don't get into a mess."

"Sorry, but I can't just walk away from this. See me tomorrow and get it over with. It won't take long."

He put on his coat and a tweed cap, and handed me a business card.

"Tomorrow at three. If you change your mind, call."

Wohl, Perillo, Friedland, and Carpenter joined us.

"We've been discussing what you said, LeVine," Perillo began. "If Walter could trust you, I guess maybe we can."

"LeVine," said Wohl, "we *are* worried about a note."

"Excuse me," Goldmark interrupted, eager to leave.

"Night folks. Milt, see you tomorrow. Everybody." He waved an undirected good-bye and slipped out the door.

"Agents," snorted Friedland.

"Larry's a good boy," Wohl said thoughtfully. "This just scared the shit out of him. Scares the shit out of me, too."

Carpenter threw his arm around me, confidential-like.

"The problem is this, LeVine, straight and simple. We are worried that Walter was the first victim of something, call it a wave of fear, that's just begun in the last month or so to infect the movie industry. If we seem concerned, maybe a little hysterical, it's because those of us who were . . ." he groped for the word, "*associated* with Walter feel that his death marks a deepening of this crisis. We sense a chill in the air."

"Does this chill have something to do with politics?" I asked. "Walter signed his name to everything but candy wrappers."

Wohl's smile was a history of regrets. "So did we all, LeVine."

"What exactly did Walter tell you when he asked you to come out here?" asked Perillo.

"That's confidential, even if he's dead now. But he basically told me very little. Just that there was some trouble he wanted me to investigate."

"And that was it?" asked Wohl.

"Just about."

"Let's not beat around the bush," Carpenter said with sudden force. "LeVine, we might need you as much as Walter did. That's why we're standing around here now, trying to figure out what was on Walter's mind. We're not ghouls. It's a practical problem we're facing. Careers are at stake."

There was much nodding of heads.

"I lived through it before," Friedland said solemnly. "Progressive people being hounded to their deaths."

Rachel Wohl came up to her husband and took his arm.

"Milt, I told the sitter we'd be back by eleven."

Wohl looked sheepish. "Children."

Friedland beamed like a Viennese Santa. "Ah, *die schönen kinder.*"

We all decided it was time to go. Carroll Arthur and his wife were going to stay overnight in case Mrs. Adrian needed anything. June Arthur was reasonably sober, but Carroll was still swimming at the deep end. Mrs. Arthur smiled at me.

"It'll be okay. Helen's a strong girl."

I told her I thought so too, and then the whole pack of us got our coats and headed outside, saying our good-byes and shaking hands. It had gotten a good deal cooler and a stiff breeze had the palms bending like catapults. I looked back at the Adrian place; the upstairs lights were still on and I guessed that Helen Adrian wasn't going to sleep well tonight. Nothing in this world is as empty as a man's house on the evening he dies. Everything in the house seems to die with him.

The cars started backing out of the driveway. I got into my Chrysler and started up. No neighbors were out. There seemed to be peace and quiet and ignorance on Escadero Road. But as I drove off I was certain that dozens of eyes were peeking through dozens of curtains.

4

The sun was beating on the curtains and a brilliant patch of dust-filled light hung over my bed, the particles tumbling silently like snow in a glass paperweight. I watched with pleasure, a child waking in his crib, snug, and yawning. I stretched and kicked the sheets. It was a quarter to seven in the morning and there was no way, save anesthesia, that I could get back to sleep. My head was busy and lucid, my stomach was roaring; against all my historic principles and precepts, I arose for the day.

A shower and shave, fresh underwear and yesterday's brown suit. Humming all the while, I tied the tie and crossed the laces, hitting the street at a quarter past, a hungry lion stalking breakfast on the veldt. The day was a gleaming beauty, heralded by a chorus of birds perched in the Real's fruit trees. Gentle sunlight and easy warmth fell on my back; I smiled at a familiar bald shadow on the pavement. On Sunset Boulevard, an elderly couple sat on a bench in the sunshine, waiting for a bus. They looked very happy. I thought about moving to L.A. then remembered the reason I was out here in the first place. But it wasn't enough to make me feel bad; I felt a certain detachment from the Adrian case. It really wasn't my problem, was it? I had found my own bit of California, if only a California of morning walks to coffee shops. I felt wonderful. It lasted almost half an hour.

Over freshly squeezed juice, scrambled eggs, hash browns, and a pot of coffee, I opened up the *Los Angeles Times* for news of Adrian's death. I figured it would be a page one item, given the bizarre circumstances, but the *Times* had the story, with a head shot of Walter, on the bottom of page three.

WALTER ADRIAN FOUND DEAD
SCREENWRITER APPARENT SUICIDE

Screenwriter Walter Adrian was found dead last night at Warner Brothers Studios in Burbank, an apparent suicide. The body of the forty-year-old Adrian, whose many credits included *Three-Star Extra, Boy From Brooklyn, Berlin Commando,* and *Beloved Heart,* was discovered by a close friend. Los Angeles Police Lieutenant George Wynn said the probable cause of death was strangulation and there was "no evidence of foul play." He would not divulge whether a note had been found.

Studio officials and friends told the *Times* that Adrian had been despondent for some time, but all were shocked at the writer's death. Said Jack Warner, "All of us at Warner Brothers mourn the tragic passing of Walter Adrian. He was a man of great character, as well as a writer of enormous skill. Millions of Americans, who loved *Three-Star Extra, Berlin Commando, Beloved Heart,* and the forthcoming Easter release, *Alias Pete Costa,* will miss him."

Adrian's long-time friend, Academy Award-winning scenarist Milton Wohl declared that "the world has lost a fighter for decency, the industry has lost a courageous and gifted voice, and I have lost a dear, dear friend."

Adrian is survived by his wife, Helen. Funeral services will be held Friday at Temple B'nai Sholom, in Beverly Hills. Persons are asked not to send flowers, but to forward contributions to the National Association for the Advancement of Colored People and the American Civil Liberties Union.

The power of the press to play things up and play things down never ceased to amaze me. The spectacular fact that Adrian had been found dangling from a gallows on the Western Street at Warners, a fact my beloved *Daily News* would have spread all over the front page, with pictures ("SCRIBE'S LAST ROUNDUP"), went unmentioned. It appeared that Warners' flaks had worked overtime, either at getting the cops to keep mum or holding their advertising power to the *Times'* throat. For myself, I was grateful to have become an anonymous "friend." The story left the unmistakable impression that all concerned were handling the matter with tongs.

When I got back to the hotel, the desk clerk handed me a piece of paper with a telephone message from Lieutenant Wynn. The message was that I was to go, immediately and directly, to his office. The half hour was up; blue skies or gray, I was a small-time shamus in a familiar creek *sans* paddle.

Wynn didn't really have an office; it was a cubicle set in a bullpen on the third floor of the downtown L.A. police headquarters, a building that would not have looked out of place in Long Island City's warehouse district. The bullpen was a long green room full of cranky homicide dicks in threadbare sports jackets and the insistent din of teletype machines and ringing telephones. Wynn's cubicle had flimsy green partition walls topped by a foot of frosted glass, but there was a good fifteen feet between the glass and the ceiling. He had a kind of privacy, but not much more than you find in the pay toilets of a metropolitan bus terminal.

"Lovely setup here," I told him.

Wynn was alone today. He chewed a pencil and surveyed me from behind a bare municipal-issue desk. "It'll do," he said. "As a matter of fact it doesn't do, but it'll have to do. So it does. Have a seat."

I perched myself on a municipal-issue chair, a straight-backed beauty with no arms and a seat treated with iron. Wynn sat swiveling back and forth in his small metal chair, never taking the pencil from his molars or his eyes away from me. It is what cops call psychology. They take courses.

"What are you trying to do," I finally said, "break me?"

"Big mouth," Wynn said softly. He stopped swiveling and leaned across the top of his desk. "A New York big mouth. We get lots of them out here, know-it-alls." He smiled at me like he knew something that I didn't. Very likely, because I didn't know a thing.

There was a rap at the door; Lemon and Caputo strolled in, bored to death, and sat down on opposite sides of Wynn's desk, like bookends. Caputo handed Wynn a manila folder. The lieutenant opened it and examined the contents very critically, very police lab. Lemon and Caputo slid off the desk and left the office.

"They're bright boys," I said. "I could use a couple like that."

Wynn ignored the remark. "LeVine, we're about to close the books on this Adrian suicide. I just want to tie it up with ribbons." He leaned back in his chair and stuck a Kaywoodie pipe between his yellow teeth. It didn't make him look anything like a Harvard professor.

"You're absolutely sure it was suicide?"

Wynn lit up, smoke billowing from both sides of his mouth. "As sure as I have to be," he said. "Your pal Adrian was as Red as a firetruck. That's why he croaked himself."

"How Red is a firetruck?"

"Very. A firetruck carries a little card in its pocket which says it thinks Russia's the greatest thing since bottled beer." His teeth clamped down hard on the stem of the pipe. "But I'm not telling you anything new."

"Walter was a Communist?"

Wynn smiled with subpolar warmth.

"Not bad, LeVine. You take acting lessons in New York?" He started leafing through his folder.

"You're going to roll on the floor, Lieutenant, but he never told me."

"The floor's too dirty," the cop said without looking up, "but imagine that I'm rolling."

Funny thing was that despite what I remembered about Walter's politics at City, and despite his disconnected remarks at Lindy's, I hadn't really figured on his joining the Party. Maybe I hadn't figured because I didn't want to, because I wanted to make the case simpler than it was, but there it was, suddenly as obvious as a cloudburst. Walter was a world-saver from day one, I knew that well enough; he wept for the ninety-nine percent of the earth's transients who got screwed from both ends and between the eyes. He'd sign anything and not ask why; he believed that his motives—concern, empathy, economic outrage—were everyone's motives. Besides which, Walter had delicate antennae for social survival; if the right people in Hollywood had begun joining the Party ranks, it probably occurred to him that following their lead would not have an adverse effect on his career. This is not to say that Walter's ideals were not genuine. It is to say that, like all of us, Walter's revolution began at home.

"What's your evidence?" I asked Wynn.

"It could fill a freight car, take my word for it."

"Your what for it? Listen, even granting the evidence, why does Walter's being a Red necessarily prove suicide?"

Wynn continued to leaf through the folder.

"It doesn't, necessarily, but in this case I believe it does."

"Why?"

"Because the word is that being a Red is going to go out of style around here, and fast."

"Another Scare?"

"Something like that. A lot of people, and some very big people, are going to get burned."

Things began falling into place. The tension among Adrian's friends, Carpenter's saying that they all might be needing help, the panicky questions about a suicide note.

Wynn broke up my line of thought. "Why did he fly you out here, LeVine?"

"He was worried."

"About what?"

I shook my head. "He's still my client. I can't tell you that."

Wynn's pipe went out. He relit it. "Okay, another tack," he said. "Was he desperately worried?"

"Not suicidally, if that's what you mean. By the way, how come a writer kills himself and there's no note? And how come there's a swelling on the back of his head like someone might have sapped him?"

Wynn waved me off. "Quit it, LeVine, you're trying too hard. Lots of suicides don't leave notes, writers and stationery salesmen included. The swelling checks out as well; he got a crack on his head going through the trapdoor."

"The door isn't that small," I told him. "And I don't figure stringing yourself up on a gallows. How can you reach the lever while standing on a trapdoor?"

Wynn stared up at a large globe light suspended from the ceiling.

"Don't have to," he said casually, distractedly. He extracted a yellow sheet from his folder. "LeVine, let me clear something up in my mind. Why did he fly you out here? Why not hire a local peeper?"

"How many times do I have to tell you that he's an old friend, that we attended . . ."

" 'In 1927,' " Wynn began reading from the yellow sheet of paper, " 'Levine's name appears on a petition in the City College of New York student newspaper, calling for a pardon in the case of Sacco and Vanzetti. In 1937, Levine, now a private investigator working under the name of LeVine,' " Wynn lifted his head and smiled, at which point I barely controlled an impulse to knock his teeth through the back of his head, " 'sent money and an offer of personal help to Spanish Refugee Aid. He repeated that offer, and forwarded another check to Spanish Refugee Aid in 1938.' " Wynn handed me the yellow sheet. "There it is, in black and white."

The sheet was a memo to Wynn from the Federal Bureau of Investigation, from Agent Clarence White.

"You request these as a matter of routine?" I asked.

"Of course not," he said sharply, "but this is a special case, highly sensitive."

"I see. So you requested that the FBI run a check on me?"

Wynn was discomfited.

"The FBI is helping us on this one."

"That's not an answer."

"You're not in a position to demand answers, Levine or Vine or whatever you call yourself. Not with an FBI file on you." He was getting pretty ugly.

"That's a file? A petition signed in '27 and two checks sent out a decade later? Come on, Wynn, you're being silly."

His broad nostrils flared, he poked a finger at his chest.

"You won't find an FBI file on George Wynn," he said proudly.

"Maybe that's because you never cared about a goddamn thing. I thought General Franco was a dog in 1937 and I still think he's a dog. Tomorrow I'll think he's a dog. Call me and I'll tell you so. As for poor old Sacco and Vanzetti, I don't remember what I thought. I was twenty-one and I didn't like to see people killed. I still don't. And I cannot believe that the FBI considers that chickenshit as worth keeping on file."

"That's not for you to judge," the lieutenant said coolly. His tone had changed. He had the goods on me, he was Mr. Prosecutor. "Are you still going to tell me that Walter Adrian hired you merely because you were a college chum?"

That was enough for me; that was plenty. I arose and started bellowing.

"Okay, Wynn, you got me dead to rights. I knew I couldn't hide it much longer from L.A. Homicide. You're too sharp for a bald Jewboy like me. Here's how it happened, but try and make it easy on me, willya? Adrian flew into New York, took a hack to my office, and slipped me the secret Red handshake. I can't reveal it to you here, even in the relative security of this office. Then he paid me three hundred bucks and expenses to fly out here. Why? *Voilà,* it's simplicity itself. Because he intended to hang himself, of course."

"Sit down," Wynn said fiercely, "or I'll throw you in the can."

"For what, the petition about killing the shoemaker and fishpeddler or the checks to the refugees?" I put on my hat and went to the door. It opened and Lemon and Caputo stood blocking my way. They grabbed me by either arm. I turned to Wynn.

"So help me Christ, these two shitheads better let go," I said in a low growl, as close to menacing as I could muster.

Wynn, in a sudden attack of intelligence, told them to leave. He snapped his fingers and they vanished.

"LeVine," he said placidly, "you're behaving very badly today."

I stood by the door.

"I don't enjoy threats, Lieutenant, but I particularly don't enjoy dumb threats. That FBI crap," I waved toward the folder, "that's an insult."

The cop puffed bleakly on his pipe and I realized the G-man routine wasn't his idea.

"You don't like it too much yourself, do you, Wynn?"

"Go back to New York," he said quietly, his eyes dull and unhappy. "We don't need you here anymore."

"That's reason enough for me to stay. I was hired to find out why Walter was in trouble. I'd still like to find out."

"You found out."

"Not good enough; I'm not satisfied."

"Sometimes you ought to be satisfied with being un-satisfied. It's part of life."

"I'm unsatisfied and leave it that way too goddamn many times. I'm tired of it."

Wynn stood up and walked to the door. He had had enough of me, enough of my mouth and enough of my doubts. There were loose ends all over the place and he knew it and couldn't do anything about it. No homicide dick enjoys that.

"Bye, LeVine," he said, opening the door. "Hope we don't have to meet again."

"I think we will."

"I think we won't. This is being put to bed. Let it sleep."

We didn't shake hands but only nodded to each other, unconvinced of each other's words and intentions. I don't think I've ever left a cop's office feeling any other way.

5

Larry Goldmark was feeling much better today. Color had returned to his cheeks and he sat behind his mahogany desk sipping a Coca-Cola and smiling. He gestured around the room with his free hand. "What a mess, huh? We've only been here three weeks."

Books and manuscripts littered the agent's desk, a coffee table, and miles of shelf space. Cardboard boxes, sealed and tied with rope, were stacked up behind a red felt-covered couch. Dark curtains shut out the afternoon sun. Goldmark caught me looking at them.

"You're having a typical New York reaction," he said cheerily. "Why live in California if you're going to keep the curtains closed, right? I'll tell you something: after a couple of months you take the sunshine for granted. I work better in the dark. Sid keeps his drapes open and that, as the man said, is what makes horse races."

Sid was Goldmark's partner in the agency, Sidney Margolies. They had relocated to a three-room suite in the La Paloma Building on Beverly Boulevard, a building as yet unfinished. Workmen still crawled around the lobby floor in white overalls. Goldmark–Margolies was one of a dozen tenants.

"We were in a tiny office on Wilshire and the lease ran out," Goldmark explained. "We had to move. I don't give a damn if the lobby isn't finished, as long as the elevator runs."

He laughed but I didn't, so he stopped.

"Business good?" I asked.

Goldmark solemnly rapped his knuckles on the desk.

"Knock wood. Like beavers. Since the war, Sid and I have built one of the most successful shops in town. And we started from scratch, I mean *scratch*."

"You mainly represent writers?"

He leaned way back in his leather recliner and stuck a polished black shoe up on his desk, careful to place the heel on a script.

"We started with only writers, but we've picked up a director or three," the agent said contentedly. "We're just starting to take off. Our growth has been terrific, considering the problems in the industry: postwar readjustment, the television scare." He broke off. "But you're not interested in that end. Let's talk detective talk."

"I'm not so hot at detective talk," I said amiably. "The guys on radio do it better. But it's nice to see you so relaxed today, Goldmark. Seemed to me you were pretty hard hit last night."

Goldmark nodded vigorously. "Absolutely, Jack. I was a man in total shock yesterday evening. Completely numb. Returning to Walter's house and remembering the good times, well . . ." His voice carefully trailed off. "To be perfectly frank with you, I just wanted to get the hell out of there. It got to me."

"I can understand that. But today you feel fine."

He tensed slightly. "Don't make it sound like a crime, pal. I'm still upset but today is today, and the big parade goes on, no?" He held out his hands in a gesture of philosophic acceptance. He understood life's mysteries and tragedies, this gold-plated putz.

"Comme ci, comme ça," he continued. "I'll level with you, Jack, if you're interested."

"Please."

"Walter was a sick man," he said, very serious and sincere now, "and he shouldn't have done what he did. It was irresponsible, to Helen, to his friends, to the industry. But it's done. You're not going to bring Walter back, I'm not going to bring Walter back. So let's go on."

"With what?"

Goldmark looked at me oddly, then his phone buzzed and he picked up. "No calls, Judy. Who? Okay." He smiled at me. "Sorry, Jack, but I've been waiting for this bum to return a call for a week."

"I understand."

"Business is business." His apologies were nonstop. Goldmark winked at me and then began hollering into the mouthpiece. "Robby, my friend. How's the boy? Darryl told me you had some kind of a flu bug. Sure, Darryl talks to me. It's all in the technique." He laughed and laughed, looking at me with a big grin as if I, too, were supposed to start guffawing. I responded by picking my teeth with my thumbnail.

"Listen, amigo, reason I called," the agent was saying, was this . . ." He stopped and rolled out the mortician's carpet. "Oh, it's awful about Walter. Crazy. But between you and me, Robby, I saw it coming for a long time. He was a very unhappy man." Goldmark paused and shook his head somberly, as if Robby could see him. "Of course he shouldn't have done it. It was irresponsible, to Helen, to his friends, to the industry. I'm sick about the whole thing. He was a client, sure, but before that, a friend." He listened a bit more and looked at his watch. "Rob, reason I called is this: Mike Adler is coming into town next Monday and would love to talk to you people about an idea he's got. You've got a call from London? Okay. Listen, you'll be at Walter's funeral tomorrow? Fine, we'll put our heads together afterwards. Love ya."

Goldmark hung up and shrugged. "Sorry, but that was Bob Lester of the Fox story department."

"I never heard of him but I'm impressed anyway. I'm impressed all the time out here."

Goldmark thought that might be a joke, so he laughed. I lit up a Lucky and went on.

"Goldmark, I get the distinct impression that you believe Walter killed himself because he was some kind of a neurotic."

"He *was* a neurotic."

"Which is why he checked himself out?"

"Correct."

"Well, that's not what the cops think."

The agent took his foot off the script on the desk and rolled his chair forward.

"They don't think it was suicide?" he whispered.

"No, they think it was suicide, all right, but they chalk it up to something besides neurosis. They are claiming that Walter killed himself because he was a Communist, card-carrying variety, and terrified that he'd be ruined by the revelation. The cops hinted that some kind of major scandal is brewing."

Goldmark's voice went as hollow as a dial tone. "Who told you that?"

"A lieutenant named Wynn, Homicide. You may be hearing from him, or maybe not. Depends on how fast he closes the books on this case."

"Case?"

"Could be a murder, you know. Let me level with you, Goldmark. Maybe you'll do the same for me."

He was leaning so far forward he was practically on the floor. "Sure Jack, what?"

"Reason I say it could be a murder is that there wasn't

any note and there was a lump on the back of Walter's head that could have gotten there in any number of ways, none of them delicate, many of them illegal."

I had no business telling Goldmark any of this, except that I entertained the logical hunch that a guy whose profession consisted almost entirely of knowing which way the winds were blowing probably knew a great deal more than he was letting on. He drummed his fingers on the desk top.

"Murder," was all he said.

"Nobody believes it, Goldmark, but it's not an impossibility."

"But the cops don't think so?"

"If they do, they're not letting on." There was also the vague matter of FBI interference, but I saw no reason to go into that. I had been open enough for one day.

"You think it's murder, Jack?"

"I don't think anything. I'm just not counting it out. The fact is that I was only hired by Walter to find out who was causing him trouble. Now that he's dead, the nature of that trouble becomes a pretty serious matter, especially if it was murder. That's what I have to figure out."

"You think I can help you?" asked the agent.

"I'm positive you can help me."

Goldmark was getting very unhappy. A film of sweat glistened on his forehead and he started slapping through his pockets in search of a cigarette. I tossed him my pack and he dropped it on the floor.

"Relax," I told him.

"You don't know what all this has meant to me. Walter's death. . . ." He shook his head and lit up.

"It hasn't been a pillow fight for anyone, Goldmark. Now, just tell me who at Warners was giving Walter a hard time."

"Johnny Parker," the agent said bleakly. "He's a V-P for production at Warners. He rides herd on the writers."

"Did he have it in for Walter? Personal grudge, anything like that?"

Goldmark thought it over, his brow furrowed behind a drifting cloud of smoke. The breezy Mr. Hollywood manner had been returned to the stage trunk.

"No," he finally said. "I really don't think so. Fact is, Parker used to socialize with the writers, with Walter and Milt Wohl. Used to kind of run in their circle. Last year or so he's changed, become more of an executive. Maybe he figured it was bad for his reputation to hang out with writers."

"When did he start making noise about the new contract?"

"Walter tell you about that, or Mrs. Adrian?" he asked guardedly.

"Walter."

He nodded. "Couple of weeks ago he started making ridiculous, insulting counteroffers. Before then he had just been stalling. It's been going on since December."

"Why the insulting offers? The cops right about the Red angle, was that it?"

Goldmark resigned himself to spilling the beans. He exhaled and placed his hands flat down on the desk. "Christ, yes, they're right. That's the whole ball of wax, Jack. You saw that bunch of people at Walter's house last night. They're terrified, quaking in their pants. Milt Wohl is coming to see me at five, just so I'll hold his hand and tell him it's going to be all right."

"Is that whole bunch Red? Wohl, Arthur, Perillo, the cowboy?"

"Carpenter?" Goldmark shrugged, suddenly cautious. "I don't know *how* Red, Jack. Truthfully. I don't know if they carry cards or what. But they sympathize, at the very least. And if you breathe a word of this conversation to anyone at all, I'll deny it. And I won't speak to you again."

"It's that bad."

"Worse. The people you met last night are all political-minded, progressive people, and the fact of the matter is that their kind of politics is going out of style around Hollywood, like a restaurant with a ptomaine rap, that fast. Apparently—and this is strictly between us and the four walls—apparently, there is going to be some kind of a congressional investigation."

"Of what?"

"Communism in Hollywood. And if in fact there is an investigation you can bet it'll be the publicity circus of all time. The new congressman from this district is a kid named Nixon—Republican, and by a beautiful coincidence he happens to be on the Un-American Activities Committee, which would be running the show." He smiled a grim and lifeless smile. "Isn't that perfect? You think a freshman congressman would mind being on the front pages every morning, asking movie stars if they know any Reds?"

"Jesus Christ," I mumbled. It appeared that LeVine had once again managed to step into a puddle and discover that the bottom lay a hundred feet below.

"Jesus H. Christ, Esquire," said the agent. "Looks like Walter was the first victim."

"Did he ever talk to you about it?"

"Indirectly." The lit cigarette in his hand described a short arc. "He tell you anything?"

"Just loose talk about a bad time for progressive-minded people. He never got specific."

"Walter didn't confide very well. It wasn't his style." The agent seemed genuinely saddened. "That's why I accept his suicide. Walter bottled things up; for him to go before a congressional committee, with newsreel cameras and radio. . . . He'd die first."

"He did die first." I stood up. "Thanks, Goldmark. See you at the funeral."

The agent arose and walked me to the door. "I'd like to help you some more, Jack, but maybe we could meet somewhere else in the future."

"You think it's that risky?"

"I don't know, maybe." He looked abashed. "I'm no

60

hero, pal. Maybe that makes me a bum and a creep in your book, but it's the truth. I have a good business here. I can't go down with these guys. I gotta keep floating."

"I understand." I did, kind of.

We shook hands. He held on to mine and squeezed my elbow. "Where do you go from here?"

"To the gallows," I told him, and left his office to examine the place where Walter had died.

It was not the best idea I ever had.

I faked my way back onto the Warners lot with the orange sticker I had been given the night before. The kid at the gate just waved me through. I drove slowly up the center strip, gawking at the daytime activity. Men pushed racks loaded down with costumes, trucks hauled props and scenery, and actors were knocking off work. It was five o'clock and I should have been doing the same. A crew of pirates emerged from a sound stage, taking off their eye patches and lighting up some smokes. They were followed by a covey of midgets in Brooklyn Dodger uniforms, a wonder to behold. I drove to the very edge of the back lot and allowed myself the not inconsiderable thrill of parking the Chrysler in an empty space reserved for John Garfield. I got out and hoofed it over to the Western Street.

It was as deserted as it had been the night before. I had expected to find actors and technicians drifting away from their day's labors, but apparently Westerns were going out of style. Everything was as it had been, including the gallows, which I had anticipated the cops might dismantle. But for the absence of the rope, it was untouched.

I walked over and began studying the area directly beneath the wooden scaffold, finding a few flecks of dried blood on some stones, but nothing else of importance. Even the stones were unimportant. They had obviously not been used as weapons, bearing no traces of violent activity. If you bash a person on the head with a rock, there is hair and unpleasantness left on that rock. And if you bash a person on the head and then drop him through a trapdoor at the wrong end of a rope, you do not deposit that rock directly below the victim's feet. It's common sense.

Directly over my head I noticed chalk scribbling on the wooden planks that constituted the gallows floor. There were check marks next to initials and letters: K.B., R., H.P., C.W., apparently left there by crew members who had erected the structure.

I climbed the wooden stairs and paced off the distance between the trapdoor and the metal lever that sprang it. Mathematical precision was not required: no man could spring the trap while standing upon it. This, of course, did not preclude someone pulling the trap beforehand and jumping through the hole. It seemed, however, an awkward way to go about ending one's life.

It was a warm afternoon and my exertions, mild as they were, had worked up my habitual veil of perspiration. I removed my jacket and observed that my white shirt was leopard-spotted with sweat stains. So I sat for a bit, on the edge of the platform, mulling over the facts of Walter's death. That note in his pocket, "Check pos. stables. Jailhouse?" He had been out here working out a scene; that was on the note he had left me, the one I found on the floor. So that was what the stables and jailhouse were probably all about. But if they were about something else? A hunch, of course, but worth five minutes of my time.

I went down the stairs and started for the rear of the jailhouse.

Someone didn't want me to go there.

The first shot went a foot over my head, but I got the point and dove into the dust, rolling over and pulling my Colt from the pocket of the jacket that was draped casually over my shoulder. Another shot slammed dully into the dust, six inches from my argyle socks. I couldn't see who was firing or figure out which direction the bullets were flying from. For all I knew a drunken extra was firing blanks, but the only way to test that theory was to get hit and it didn't seem worth the bother. I didn't believe it was a drunken extra anyway; I figured the shots had something to do with a private detective snooping around the scene of what I, at this moment, knew to be a crime.

A third shot blew a brief gust of wind past my right ear. All I could do with my gun was exhibit it; I still didn't know where my attacker was perched. There wasn't much to do but run or get killed. Or both.

I jumped to my feet and went behind the gallows, just to put something between me and the artillery. Another shell blew past, but this one wasn't even close. I stood squinting into the sun, which was low in the sky and directly in my eyes, and determined that the shots were coming from the rear of the Frontier Hotel. If I could cut across the street, my friend's angle would be lost. Besides which, I was fairly certain that a person could not indefinitely fire bullets in a movie studio without arousing a certain degree of curiosity.

Both those assumptions proved correct. I aimed a shot at the general direction of the hotel and sprinted across the street, fleeing two more salvos, one of which came terribly close to making a puree of my brains, the other of which, my attacker's angle gone, went off an abutment on the side of the jailhouse. I reached the saloon and sailed through the swinging doors, landing on my belly, the wooden floor rattling my incisors.

I lay there, panting and listening to my heart pound, first like the rhythm section of a doped-up Latin dance band, losing a couple of beats to a rapid and blooded onetwoonetwo, and finally ebbing to normal like a breaker crashing and meshing flat and foamy into a gray winter sea. Back to life's fundamental, stately rhythms. One–two, one–two.

The shooting had stopped and I heard people running up the street outside. There was confused conversation, largely incomprehensible to me, but the gist was, what the hell's going on, shooting? The words hardly mattered; what did matter was that I didn't want to go out on the street and answer any questions, or be subjected to another tedious session with the law. There was, fortunately, a way to get out of the saloon without having to appear on the Western Street, a rear exit to a short alley adjacent to the Small-Town America lot. I crawled through the saloon on hands and knees, emerging dusty but pleased to have escaped, not merely alive but undetected. I slapped the grime off my clothing, returned the Colt to its designated pocket, and started back for the car, curiously pleased to have had my suspicions confirmed: I was working on a flesh-and-blood case, not merely a post-mortem.

I had secretly hoped that John Garfield would be standing next to the Chrysler, waiting to bawl me out for stealing his space. Garfield was absent, but a half-naked young man in a feathered headdress, loincloth, and war paint was seated on the car's back fender, studying a script.

"Hey, Chief," I called. "Beat it."

The young man was startled. "Is this your car?" he asked.

"That's right."

"Oh, I'm sorry." A smile showed off his expensive cap job. "I got so wrapped up in this grotesque script. I don't even have lines. I stand around and look noble, but *that* I do beautifully."

"I can imagine."

"I sure can." He looked me over. "Want to get a drink, handsome?"

He slid off the fender very slowly, the loincloth riding up. Apparently some kind of Indian love call. It was at this point that I noticed a deeply tanned man getting into a very impressive black Rolls-Royce. He looked to be in a hurry. I checked out the license plates; they were under glass and read JOHNPARKER. Johnny Parker.

"What do you say," the Indian brave repeated, "a great big drink?"

"Gotta run, Chief." I trotted across the street and leaned in through the window of the long black Rolls. The tanned man was settling into the driver's seat.

"You Johnny Parker?"

The man looked at me in amazement, as if the question was an unfamiliar one. His hair was coal-black and slicked back with so much Wildroot that I could see my reflection in his temples. He had watery blue eyes and a schoolboy's snub nose. The mouth was weak and unpleasant, the chin contained a dimple. He did not look like a kind man.

"I'm him," he said curtly. "Who are you?"

"Jack LeVine."

He started the engine.

"I don't know you, Mr. LeVine, and I have an appointment at six. Speak to my secretary if you wish to see me."

"I'm the guy who found Walter Adrian's body here last night, Parker, and I'd like to talk to you about it."

He shut off the engine and stared at me.

"Mind if I get in the front seat?" I asked. "I feel like a goddamn highway cop talking to you like this."

"Of course." He leaned across the front seat and unlocked the door. I circled the car and got inside. It was quite a masterpiece. The dashboard was ebony, deeply oiled, and the seats were upholstered in what felt like kid. They were colored terra-cotta and could be raised, lowered, and do flips at the touch of a switch. Parker pressed a little button near the door and his seat reclined so that he lay back like a man enjoying a Florida sunbath. A telephone had been installed in a raised center panel. It rang. Parker pushed the button again and the seat righted itself.

"Yes?" he said authoritatively into the phone. Then he listened, looking from me to his watch. He was putting on a pretty good show. "No, I'm leaving," he said. "I'm late as it is. Tell Cagney's people we'll talk about it tomorrow. The hell with it. Tomorrow at eleven, with Jimmy. I want him there, tell them that. Check." He hung up and rode his seat back down again.

"Okay, LeVine, what's the problem?"

"No problem at all. I just got curious about a couple of items concerning Adrian's status here at Warner's."

"Shoot." If he had any apprehensions about speaking with me, they did not register on his face. It was as expressionless as a cheesecake.

"Why were you out to get him?"

"Me personally?" He shook his head to indicate disbelief. "I had nothing but admiration for him. As a writer, that is. As a person to deal with, Walter could be a royal pain in the ass. But he was a vital and creative screenwriter and his death is a terrible blow to the studio." Parker wasn't crude enough to feign grief; his words echoed the corporate line on Adrian's demise.

"Then why were you raking him over the coals on his new contract?"

"Because that's the name of the game, LeVine. You can't roll over and play dead when a writer and his agent demand a thousand-dollar-a-week raise. He was demanding four thousand dollars a week. That's a lot of money anyplace, even Hollywood."

"He told me thirty-five."

Parker shrugged.

"Maybe that's what he told you. From Warner Brothers he wanted four. That was too damn much and I told him so."

"I've been told that you proposed a thousand-dollar-a-week cut in pay."

"Bullshit," he said firmly. "The truth, Mr. LeVine, is not to be found from the lips of agents." He smiled. "I should know, I used to be one myself. The fact is that I told Adrian's people that I would extend his contract for another two years, with his salary the same, twenty-five hundred a week. He was worth that much and no more."

Parker leaned toward me: the smell of cologne was strong enough to make my eyes tear. "Whatever anyone else may tell you, including his cockamaymie agent, that was the deal. The days of the five-grand-a-week writer are over, if I have any say in the matter. And I do. Let me show you something, LeVine, you strike me as a bright guy."

The executive leaned over and opened a briefcase, which was on the floor in the back. He removed a mimeographed report, its multicolored pages stapled together, and tossed it in my lap. The cover read "Television: Projections, 1947–1957." I leafed through it and saw a lot of numbers.

"This is just farina to me, Parker," I told him.

He flashed a grim smile. "To an outsider, it's nothing but dry figures. To the movie industry, it's a death sentence. That report, Mr. LeVine, projects that by the mid-1950s, something like thirty million homes, maybe more, will be equipped with television sets. And what that means is that unless we stop serving up the same tired old crap, we're going to be in serious trouble. Television will be for free, movies cost money. It's that simple."

"This is very interesting, but I'm here to talk about Walter Adrian."

"It's intimately connected, LeVine. We've got to start cutting down on our overhead here, which means that we don't pay writers whatever sky-high figures their agents talk them into demanding. Which is why we were haggling with Walter, not trying to persecute him. Period, end of speech. Anything else? I've really got to get moving." He started fingering the ignition switch.

"Two more questions. Quickies. First, the police think Walter killed himself because of his politics and the possibility they might be becoming unpopular, even professionally dangerous. Did Walter's being a little on the rosy side have anything to do with the contract crunch?"

"No," Parker said coolly. "I'm in the movie business, not the politics business. If politics were important, Walter and a lot of other people would have been out on their butts long ago. Political leanings aren't a big secret out here." He smiled ruefully. "Nothing's a big secret out here."

"If you say so. I'm just thinking that politics may stay constant, but their acceptability changes. But I'll take your word for it."

Parker lit up a thin cigar and nodded.

"My second question is a bit more personal," I continued. "How come somebody just tried to kill me for nosing around the Western Street?"

Parker went as white as a priest's ass. The cigar froze to his thumb and index finger as if soldered there, and he blinked five times in rapid succession. His eyes iced over into tiny blue discs.

"Kill you?" he managed to say. "Here on the lot?"

"Right here in movieland. I was walking from the gallows to the jailhouse when an unidentified cowpoke started shooting at me."

"You're sure it wasn't some extra fooling around with blanks?" Parker asked, trying to regain his footing. "People pull all kinds of idiot stunts around here."

"I'm sure of it. This was for real."

"Well, I'm dumbfounded, LeVine. It's ghastly." The blood had returned to his face and he was in the fight, jabbing and dancing, trying to stay off the ropes. "You must go to the police with this."

I shook my head.

"No thanks. Police think it's legal to shoot at private dicks."

"Then I'll have studio security look into it. This can't just be ignored." He held out his hand. "I have to go, LeVine. If you need any help, anything at all, feel free to call my office. If I'm not available, I'm sure my secretary will be able to help. This has been a terrible event for the studio; let's get it aired and put to rest."

"Thanks for the help, Parker." I clasped his moist hand and departed from the Rolls. "Thing is, though," I said through the window, "I can't help feeling that maybe Walter was murdered."

The executive assumed the pose of a man thinking it over. "I can't accept that, LeVine, but let's see what you can come up with. If you find something, come straight to me."

He started his car and rolled through the kingdom of Warners, an earl perhaps, or a duke. And a man who probably held the key to the Adrian case.

I watched him go and returned to my car. It was time to have dinner with Helen Adrian and persuade her to allow me to continue investigating her husband's death. I drove into yet another dazzling and heartbreaking California sunset, aware that I was more than a little excited about seeing Mrs. Adrian, and that my reasons were not entirely professional.

6

She greeted me at the door in a plain black dress, tied tightly at the waist with a knotted cord, its sleeves draped like wings from her thin arms. A single strand of pearls graced her neck, and seashell earrings clung softly to her lobes. She looked wonderful, much too wonderful. Her eyes were clear and her smile radiant, as if the storm, surprisingly, had passed. Immediately following a great loss, there is a half-world of recovery, in which the survivor is amazed at how well she, let's say, is taking the blow. The survivor does not realize that numbness has insulated her from her own feelings, that the emotional circuits have gone dead. When that numbness lifts and the circuits are restored, the pain hits very hard. I guessed that to be the case with Helen Adrian. And I was wrong. Not very wrong, but wrong enough. The lady did not fit into the predictable stages of grief.

"It's so good to see you, Jack." She hugged me tightly enough for me to say hello to a fairly spectacular body.

"Lots of visitors?"

"Endless," she said, taking my hat and tossing it in the

closet. We walked into the living room. I turned down her offer of a drink; she contented herself with some sherry.

"First, it was impossible to get the Arthurs out of here." She plopped herself comfortably onto the couch and patted a cushion to indicate that I should sit beside her. I did so.

"It was kind of them to stay, I thought, although they were both pretty loaded," I said, moving a respectable distance from the lady, who took no notice.

"It was very kind, yes, and they were very loaded, yes," she said. "If they hadn't stayed, I probably would have gone to the Wohls' house. I could not have stayed here alone last night. But the problem was that the Arthurs were in worse shape than I was, drunk and terrified. This morning we all had a little breakfast: Carroll was hung over and morose, while June kept staring at me, waiting for the hysterics to begin."

She smiled and I smiled with her. Maybe she was a little too steady a little too quickly, but what a broad.

"So I cleared them out as fast as possible," she continued, kicking off her shoes and curling her feet beneath her. "But then the phone wouldn't stop and people kept arriving, bringing enough food for the proverbial regiment. A lot of fruit baskets, but I wouldn't accept them. Ever since my mother died when I was eleven, I've associated fruit baskets with death. They're well meant but they turn a house into a funeral parlor, don't you think?"

"It's a matter of taste. But I've never really lost anybody, not through death, that is, nobody close. My folks are still alive and well; I'm no expert on family tragedy."

"God, I am." There was no bitterness in the voice, no self-pity. "My mother, cancer. I was eleven, like I said. My father remarried, to a nice lady who talks too much," she smiled, "like me. He had a heart attack last year, hung on for a couple of weeks, long enough for me to get back to Utica and see him, then died. My older brother Steven, Steven Fletcher, got killed at Anzio. Now this."

A silence joined us together. Some silences separate

people, others bring them closer. They fill in the blanks and the blanks mesh into an intuitive feeling for one another. It's almost sensual.

"You're a strong woman, Mrs. Adrian."

She nodded distantly.

"I know, but I'm tired of it." She caressed and tousled her long red hair. "Being strong has a lot of drawbacks; everybody relies on you to be this unshakable, unbreakable *thing*. It's not even human. And you feel like really collapsing, just once, just going prostrate and having someone else do the supporting. My whole marriage was like that; this is just its logical extension." She pursed her lips and raised her eyebrows, as if anticipating a question about her marriage. She got one.

"The marriage was bust?"

"Not a bust, just poor. We probably would have gone on for a while longer. I don't really know." She took a hefty sip of sherry. "I didn't want to press him, he was so moody, so fragile. That's why no one questions his suicide; Walter was such a likely candidate. One day he'd feel invincible, the next day he'd be the low man on the Hollywood totem, an outcast. Back and forth, up and down. His insecurity affected the tone of the whole marriage, of course. And our conjugal bed was less than a triumph."

She searched my face for a reaction. I wasn't sure I wanted to hear about the midnight failings of Walter Adrian and began to suspect that Helen Adrian had been hitting the sherry since high noon. Or maybe it was a symptom of shock: the defenses had crumbled and now all secrets were up for auction, lowest bids accepted.

"How long were you married?"

"Two years. We met in New York. I was working for a publisher, he came in with a manuscript, et cetera." She did not tell the story as if recounting a fairy tale. In fact, she did not tell the story at all; instead, she smiled at me and asked if I was hungry.

72

"Famished," I said.

That made her very happy.

"Marvelous." She stood up, and I with her. "I'd never know whether Walter would be voracious or wouldn't touch a thing. Made him hard to cook for." On this, her voice went as wobbly as a warped record and her eyes abruptly filled with tears. Mrs. Adrian grabbed onto me and wept, from woe, guilt, and too much sherry. I'm a good person to cry on: my shoulder is absorbent and my legs are strong. I can stand all day.

The tears went on for a while, maybe five minutes. A woman in a maid's outfit poked her head out from the kitchen. I gave her a reassuring nod and she withdrew from the room.

"Why am I criticizing Walter?" wailed Mrs. Adrian. "There was so much pressure on the guy. And now he's dead and I'm carping and bitching . . ." She couldn't continue, but went down in the surf again.

"You're the one who's under pressure now, Mrs. A." I held her and let her cry. It is not easy to hold someone who looks like Helen Adrian without feeling emotions and physical sensations somewhat stronger than pity and consolation, but I reined myself in. She was a confusing woman, and confusing women have always been my weakness, my Achilles' gland.

Mrs. Adrian's cry left her refreshed and enlivened, as if she had taken a shower. She retired to the bathroom to blot out and cosmeticize her grief, returning with the well-brushed and high-cheekboned poise of a fashion model. In a way, Helen was very much like Walter: her changes in mood were mercurial and quirky, her switches in tempo deceptive and frequent. But Walter's tempers and humors were transparent, rooted in his need for respect. His wife was surer in her footing; the shifts in mood seemed to have their basis in changing frequencies that only she could receive. She could make you crazy.

We sat down to a relaxed and delicious dinner, prepared by the maid, who was introduced to me as Mrs. Billy, a German woman in her fifties who cooked and cleaned for the Adrians three times a week. The menu consisted of a vichyssoise, pot roast with green beans and baked potatoes, and a green salad. I did most of the eating. Dessert followed: lemon cream, very strong coffee, and a story about a detective who got shot at while looking at a gallows. Mrs. Adrian was neither alarmed nor surprised by my tale; she nodded gravely and helped herself to cream and sugar.

"Jack, it confirms that Walter was murdered." She accepted my Lucky and gentlemanly light.

"Undoubtedly, Mrs. Adrian, but where do we go from here? It has to be your decision: do we keep on investigating or get out before we get hurt?"

She clasped my wrist with long, strong fingers. "We must see it through, Jack, for all kinds of reasons. If someone could kill Walter and attempt to kill you, it leaves me as the next target. As long as I have suspicions, I'm a threat to the killer, isn't that so?"

"Not necessarily. If I go back to New York, he'll know that you've called it off."

She shook her head. "That's out of the question."

She did not want to hear differently and I couldn't blame her. Personal fear wasn't the motive, it was something simple, ancient and biblical: revenge. And you can't argue against revenge.

"There's something else, Jack," she continued. "Walter's associates in his work . . ."

"You mean his political associates, the crowd that was here last night?"

She hesitated. "I'm not sure we're talking about the same thing."

"Mrs. Adrian, I am aware of the fact that Walter was a Communist, and that the people who gathered here last night are also. Am I correct?"

"Yes, you are."

"What about you?"

She cocked her head, as if thinking about the question and then as if thinking about something else, pre-Walter, pre-Hollywood. Helen Adrian floated from the room at that moment, sailing out of 1947 and into an earlier, easier time and place. She was so beautiful then, so serene, that it almost scared me. Me, a tough guy.

Helen Adrian finally said that no, she had never joined up. "I was sympathetic, but I'm no joiner."

"Did you feel pressure to join?"

"A little."

"From Walter?"

"No, Walter never pressured me to join, never. In fact, I think he was actually getting tired of the Party, not the politics, I think, so much as the meetings and the back-biting and suspicions, particularly recently."

"Who did pressure you?"

She sifted through the blue haze that screened her face, as if trying to spell out an answer in smoke.

"I didn't mean pressure like anyone giving me ultimatums, Jack. It was more in the nature of suggestion."

"By whom?"

She smiled.

"You're a persistent s.o.b."

"I'm not doing it for abstract reasons, Mrs. Adrian, believe me."

"Call me Helen, please."

"Fine, Helen. I'm asking about these people because I'm undertaking the investigation of a first-degree murder that everyone thinks was a suicide and I'm undertaking it almost completely without information or leads, three thousand miles from my home base. That is to say, three thousand miles from any cops or reporters that I know, or any hatcheck girl or hotel dick or barber who I can depend on to tell me things on the level and on time. Out here, I can only trust you and the palm trees. So I've got to press you,

Helen. Even if my questions seem pointless, give me an answer if you've got one or part of one."

Mrs. Adrian sat up in her chair and stared down at the tablecloth, pushing some crumbs around.

"You're a hundred percent right, Jack. Forgive the coy remarks. Pressure." She thought it over and furrowed her brow into soft wrinkles. "The Wohls, Milton and Rachel. Henry, Henry Perillo. He's the most organization-minded of the group, the most disciplined. He felt it compromised a member's effectiveness not to have his spouse in with him. We had arguments about it, friendly ones. He's not a bad egg."

"Did Walter talk openly about his tiring of the Party?"

"No, at least not to me. But I could see it in his face, in his expression after a meeting, in little remarks he made."

"Did he ever talk to the others about leaving?"

"In the group? I'd be surprised if he had. It would have been out of character for him to be that open about it. Besides which, Party discipline really discourages that kind of faltering and egoism." Her smile was that of the disinterested observer. "They're all in such a bind. They sit in their offices writing bilge for the big screen, bilge indistinguishable from that written by the right-wingers across the hall, except that once in a while they work into the speech of some minor character a pitch for democracy or brotherhood or working-class rights—and then they think they've really advanced the cause. And they're making these incredible amounts of money, but when they meet as progressives, they see themselves merely as ants in the anthill of Party unity, workers just like the men who bring their lunch pails to the factory everyday and make eighty cents an hour. Kind of contemptible, when you think about it. I tried not to. None of them saw the irony."

"Did Walter?"

"No. He sometimes pretended that he did, but in his gut he didn't. He wanted his status and parking space and hundred-fifty grand like everyone else. I never knew any-one who worried about money as much as Walter did."

Her eyes got a little wet and then the maid came in to clear the dishes. We got up and started for the living room, but Mrs. Adrian suddenly turned and told me to follow her. We went up the stairs.

The master bedroom was across from the top of the stairs. Mrs. Adrian walked past it and down a hallway that went back to the front of the house. We came to a study, a small, cozy room containing a couch, desk, typewriter and floor-to-ceiling bookshelves. Above the desk were framed, glossy photographs inscribed to Walter: from Mervyn LeRoy, the director, from Edward G. Robinson ("To Walter, a great writer. With affection, Eddie"), from Claudette Colbert, Humphrey Bogart, Joan Blondell, and John Garfield, dressed as a boxer. ("To Walter, a real fighter. Your dear pal, Julie.")

"I want you to stay here with me," Mrs. Adrian said very softly.

I turned to face her. Her cheeks were slightly flushed.

"In this room, I meant, Jack." She pointed to the couch. "That folds out. It's really more comfortable than the bed in the guest room. Walter slept here sometimes, when he had to work late and didn't want to disturb me coming into the bedroom. In the morning I'd find him curled on the couch in his underwear, his clothes piled up on the type-writer." She smiled, really glowed, I thought, for the first time in discussing her husband. It was as if her fondest memory of Walter was of his sleeping in another room, down a long hallway from her.

"Why do you want me to stay here?" I asked.

"It's cheaper than the hotel and mainly I'm too fright-ened right now to stay here alone. You're a detective, you know your way around guns, you're familiar with danger. That's true, isn't it? It's not just from the radio. You have faced danger, I assume?"

"Once in a while. Not daily, but enough. Too much."

She was satisfied.

"Good, then. You'll stay."

We looked at each other for a long moment. I could hear the leaves hissing in the full trees outside.

"You'll stay," Helen Adrian said, "until we learn what really happened to Walter."

"And then?"

"And then I suppose you will return to New York and I will figure out what to do with the rest of my life." She nodded abruptly and started acting the busy housekeeper, the decision made. "But first things first. I'll put fresh linen on the bed here and you can go back to the Real and get your belongings. You know how to get there from here? Want me to go with you?"

"That's okay," I said. "I'll find it."

"Fine."

I stood there looking more than a little ridiculous. This was not the kind of thing I handled well. Helen Adrian knew it. She smiled mischievously.

"Jack, no one will talk. They know you're a detective. If they do talk, the hell with them. Now get your stuff. Mrs. Billy will stay till you come back."

I stood a bit more, searching for excuses not to stay, excuses motivated by guilt at having the hots for my dead friend's wife and fear that we were both in serious danger and sitting ducks in this big rich house. Then Mrs. Adrian stepped forward and kissed me, an ambiguous peck that landed at a point equidistant to my sensual wet lips and my scratchy cheek. Then she walked out and headed for a hall closet, probably the linen closet, calling "See you later" over her shoulder.

I retrieved my gear from the Real and returned to the Adrian house about eleven. Mrs. Billy opened up and informed me that Mrs. Adrian had retired for the night.

I went upstairs and checked into the study. The bed had been made. There was a note on the pillow reading "Jack

—You'll never know how much I appreciate this. You're a wonderful man. H. A." I folded the note and put it into my suitcase, beneath the shirts. Don't say I'm not sentimental. Then I undressed and got into bed, pulling a bound script of Walter's from one of the shelves. It was *Boy From Brooklyn*. After a few pages, I got tired and doused the light, then lay there listening for the telltale squeak of a hall floorboard. A part of me, a ridiculous part, said that Helen Adrian was going to rap softly on my door and float in, a dim figure in a sheer negligee, her body's shadows a mystery of the night. An imperceptible hitch of her shoulders and the gown would billow to the floor. Naked, oiled, perfumed, she would slip into bed to straddle me and drive us both through a midnight of slow pleasures.

I stood sentinel by my hopes for an hour or two, wondering all the time if I should be the aggressor and go creeping into her tent. Perhaps she was keeping watch also.

My waking grew choppy, with blind spots of time that must have been sleep. I yielded and turned over, bothered by something I had to do tomorrow but could not locate. Finally I found it.

At ten o'clock I had to be at Walter's funeral.

7

I t was an interesting funeral. Five hundred mourners filled Temple B'nai Sholom in Beverly Hills, a ritzy edifice to a sun-tanned God who knew how to look the other way. I say "mourners" in a purely descriptive sense, for there was very little weeping or wailing. The dominant emotion was uneasiness.

From my seat in the last row I could barely see Helen. Her features were veiled and indecipherable. Walter's sister and brother-in-law had come in from Chicago and sat looking pale, rumpled, and out of place amid the expensively tailored Californians, craning their necks to spot celebrities. Walter's mother had decided to remain in New York and was spending the day bent over double in a storefront synagogue in Brooklyn. And that was where Walter's funeral was really taking place today, in the back row of a freezing shul.

The God who presided over Beverly Hills—Our Father Who Art in Technicolor—couldn't be bothered with old ladies. This God mingled with the great and blessed their tennis courts and kidney-shaped pools. Among his worshippers today were John Garfield, Barbara Stanwyck, Humphrey Bogart, Karen Morley, Edward G. Robinson, and Lloyd Nolan. Jack Warner was there, wearing a red skullcap, seated next to Johnny Parker, whose eyes darted continuously about the room, alighting always on his watch. When Parker stood, he swayed from foot to foot. He was nervous, he wanted out, and I guessed he had an appointment. Parker's discomfiture intrigued me, and having nothing better to do, I decided to follow him after the services. I would tail him, and tail him good, until I was satisfied that he either was or wasn't a major player in this case.

The funeral proceeded apace. A young rabbi named Zalman Winkler presided and spoke of Walter as a "heroic Jewish artist, of imagination and conscience," one who "brought his imagination to the celluloid universe of film." He managed to get in a plug for Walter's last picture, *Alias Pete Costa,* saying that it was "due for release at that sacred time when we celebrate another release, that of the Jews from Egypt, that is to say, Pesach." Jack Warner nodded solemnly at the rabbi's words. After working in a few more parallels between the picture business and the flight of the Hebrews, all of which led to the inescapable conclusion that Moses had shepherded his people directly to the Brown Derby, Rabbi Winkler mercifully stopped and introduced Dale Carpenter.

The actor stepped to the lectern and removed a sheet of paper from a black leather slipcase. It was a Wordsworth poem, "At The Grave of Burns," which he read with considerable feeling, particularly its closing stanzas:

> For he is safe, a quiet bed
> Hath early found among the dead,
> Harboured where none can be misled,
>   Wronged, or distrest;
> And surely here it may be said
>   That such are blest.

And oh for Thee, by pitying grace
Checked oft-times in a devious race
May He, who halloweth the place
    Where Man is laid
Receive thy Spirit in the embrace
    For which it prayed!

Sighing I turned away; but ere
Night fell I heard, or seemed to hear,
Music that sorry comes not near,
    A ritual hymn,
Chanted in love that casts out fear
    By Seraphim.

Carpenter stepped from the lectern. Rabbi Winkler then introduced Milton Wohl and Henry Perillo, who delivered two very personal, and very revealing eulogies.

The writer went first, speaking in a voice that started at a quaver and then evened out into a mournful and resonant sing-song. "What about us, the survivors of yet another loss," said Wohl. "How do we learn from the tragic circumstances of our good friend Walter's death? How do we, workers in an industry whose products attempt to profess the humanistic values of decency, freedom of thought, and brotherhood, learn to apply those values to ourselves and the way we live? How do we come to love, trust, and help each other more?" I heard some coughing and scanned the room. Edward G. Robinson sat with his head bowed and his arms folded across his chest, Jack Warner was gazing up at the ceiling, Johnny Parker was checking the time.

"Walter," Wohl continued, "you were a hell of a writer, and a fighter for the betterment of the common lot of mankind. We've all been asking ourselves why your life had to end so abruptly, with so many triumphs still before you. Well, maybe it was a warning to us all, Walter, a warning to get our houses in order. To stop suspecting our neighbors and friends, to devote ourselves to a kinder and saner world, where our work will be a reflection of the best in us, a world in which future Walter Adrians will be free to write as honestly and bravely as the limits of their creativity will allow. I think that's what you would have wanted your friends and co-workers to think today. I know you would not have wanted us to be angry, because anger was not in you. You were a rare one, Walter, and it was a joy to spend part of the journey with you." Wohl's voice broke on his last words and he left the lectern wiping his eyes with a blue handkerchief.

Perillo followed, wearing a black woolen suit that looked as if it had been suspended in a bag full of mothballs for the past ten years. He marched to the lectern, took some pages from a slipcase, placed the case on the floor by his feet, and donned a pair of steel-rimmed spectacles. Without looking up, he cleared his throat and began reading from his paper.

"This is a day rich with meaning for the industry in which many of us are employed. A tragedy has befallen one of us, and all of us. I convey my deepest sympathies to the Adrian family, especially to Helen, and assure them that these sympathies are felt by my brothers in the International Alliance of Theatrical Stage Employees. And more than sympathy. Anger." He looked up, his eyes burning behind the specs. "Deep anger at the events and the climate in this industry that led to the passing of our dear Walter Adrian.

"We are coming to a crossroads. Much has been whispered about in the privacy of our homes. Rumors fly, accusations are passed from ear to ear. Let us voice this openly now, let us bring our concern into focus. Is the death of Walter Adrian just the first casualty in a war between the progressive-minded men and women of the movie industry and reactionary lackeys who seek to turn the clock back to the Stone Age?" Perillo thumped his hand on the lectern and people began to stir. I saw Bogart turn to Garfield and raise his eyebrows. Parker sat staring at his feet.

"Is Walter Adrian," Perillo continued, gaining in speed and volume, "the first sacrifice to a clique of reactionary congressmen who hope to fatten themselves off a fearful movie industry, one that thrives on popular acceptance, one whose economic well-being hangs on a slender thread of respectability and imagined 100 percent Americanism? Are the progressive-minded workers of the industry going to hide in their houses and surrender their cherished beliefs in the freedom and dignity of all men, regardless of race or color? I say no! I say Walter Adrian did not die, so that his friends might succumb to an orgy of fear and sterile self-criticism! Let us never imagine that we can compromise on the issues over which we have fought so long and so well. There is no compromise, only capitulation!

"No, Walter's death will not be wasted on his friends. Ever more vigilant of our freedoms and the safeguards of our treasured Constitution, we shall burn the candles late into the night. We shall watch over our rights and principles like a mother over a feverish infant. That is what Walter Adrian would have wanted from his friends and that is what Walter Adrian will get from his friends!"

Perillo turned and walked away, stuffing his speech into his pocket and removing his spectacles. There followed an absolutely tubercular explosion of coughing, a violent clearing of a hundred congested throats. Rabbi Winkler, looking as comfortable as an asthmatic deep-sea diver, returned to the lectern and led a closing invocation. As he did, I saw Parker whisper into Jack Warner's ear and start edging out into the aisle, nodding at acquaintances as the invocation ended and Walter's coffin was borne out a side door. I watched it go, watched Helen follow the casket with a bowed head, and then flew out the back door and into the parking lot.

The limousines were lining up for the trip to the cemetery. Helen and Walter's sister and brother-in-law headed for the lead limo, the Wohls, the Arthurs, and Goldmark were climbing into the second one, while Carpenter, Perillo, and Friedland entered the third. Other luminaries stood waiting, but Johnny Parker was already backing his Rolls out of a space between two Cadillacs. I raced for the Chrysler and climbed inside as Parker started out of the lot. The engine took a maddening while to turn over, during which time the Rolls was making its somber and dignified way onto Wilshire Boulevard. Fate ran Parker into a red light and I was able to find a cozy little niche about four cars in back of him. There was very little chance of losing the executive in traffic; his Rolls was as conspicuous as a white whale.

We stayed on Wilshire for miles and miles. Occasionally I'd get beaten through a light, but there was never a cause for panic. Parker had given no indication of spotting me; in fact, he was driving with the caution of a man who didn't want to attract attention. He went on and on, at a steady forty miles per hour, out of Beverly Hills and past Hancock Park, more miles east, still traveling at a measured pace, taking the bend around Hoover Street, past the hospital and into the shabby downtown area. I remained three cars behind and tailed Parker around Pershing Square, a rundown playground for derelicts and hustlers.

Parker took a left on Hill, a right on Fourth, crossed San Pedro, and finally hooked a short left onto an unpromising dead end with the Turkish monicker of Omar Avenue. He pulled up to the curb in front of something called the Pill Building, a shabby, gutted five-story mousetrap that yearned for a wrecker's ball. Parker got out of the Rolls. He looked at the building and then at the car, in a worrisome, agitated manner, as if concerned for its safety or, perhaps, visibility. Omar Avenue was a very dead end with a boarded-up diner and shuttered pharmacy and a dingy beauty parlor with yellowing photographs of prehistoric hairstyles in the window, the kind of parlor that serviced old ladies or maybe people who placed bets on horse races. Omar Avenue was not used to Rolls-Royces, but there wasn't a goddamn thing Parker could do about it, so he locked up and disappeared inside the Pill Building.

I had pulled up in back of a parked Hudson on Fourth Street and was getting out, when a blue Pontiac raced past me and took the turn on Omar very sharply, stopping abruptly in front of the Pill Building. I ducked behind my car and observed two men emerge from the Pontiac. They were both in their early thirties. One was wearing sunglasses, a natty blue sports jacket, and wheatcolored slacks. His hair was clipped very short. The other guy needed a shave and was attired in a suit of such a peculiar cut that it looked to have the wooden hangers and paper stuffing still inside. He had a curiously baby face behind the growth of beard, with an infant's fatty jowls and the thick eyebrows of an adolescent who had been carpeted with body hair overnight. Most prominent on his pale face was a nose that went down and then abruptly out, like a Rockaway shoot-the-chute. He stood jiggling on the balls of his feet, punching one hand lightly into the other.

The natty man with the small mouth leaned in through the window of the blue Pontiac and spoke to the driver, a heavy-set type with a gray fedora pulled way down on his forehead. The fedora nodded, then drove down the street and out of view. The two men stood on the sidewalk and gazed at the yellow building for an uncertain moment; then the one with the crewcut nudged the one with the eyebrows and they walked inside.

I straightened up and got out from behind the Chrysler, heading down Fourth and across Omar. I walked carefully up to the Pill Building and peered through a fly-stained pane of glass wedged loosely in a splintery door. The door said "Fuck You" in lipstick. Through the smeared glass, I saw the two men waiting, silhouetted against a window at the end of the narrow, unlit lobby. Their faces were dimly illuminated by the opening of elevator doors. They

86

got aboard, the doors closed, and I cautiously entered the building.

The lobby of the Pill Building couldn't have passed inspection in Calcutta. Part of the fake marble wall was decayed away, leaving in its wake a dangling vine of exposed electrical wiring. A phone booth next to a stairwell was gutted and urinous, the receiver swinging ghost-like in the draft caused by the opening and closing of the front door. The lobby floor was filthier than the men's room of a nuthouse: cigarette butts and candy wrappers had been stamped flat and black. Scattered beneath the stairs were newspapers and ancient, discarded condoms, aged as brittle as stemware. They lay unattended, coffins of the unborn, wreathed by garlands of dust.

Across from the elevator was a ruined directory. Letters and numbers were missing in profusion, leaving a pathetic, gap-toothed shorthand: "Abramtz, Dentit," "Nelson & elo, eal Esta." There were a couple of novelty firms, Royal Publishing Co., and a sprinkling of chiropractors, appraisers, and lawyers who chased the lawyers who chased the ambulances.

The elevator had stopped at four.

I raced silently up the stairs, taking them two at a time. I stopped on the landing below the fourth floor and heard a door closing at the end of the hall, then continued on up. The hall was very long, wide and high-ceilinged, like that of a municipal hospital. As in the lobby, there was only the natural light of an open window; the electrical fixtures had all burned out, bulb by bulb, like the tenants of the Pill Building.

A light went on behind a closed door. I tiptoed down the hall and flattened myself next to the occupied office. The frosted glass on the door read "S. Haller, Antiques and Jewelry Appraised." I heard voices.

"Johnny, good to see you," a voice said. "Hope this isn't an inconvenience."

"Certainly not. Anyway I can help." Parker sounded strained.

"Have you ever met the congressman?"

"No, I haven't, Davis, but I've heard marvelous things about him."

"Well, let's get on with it," jollied the first voice. "Johnny Parker, meet Congressman Dick Nixon."

"I've enjoyed your movies greatly," said a third voice, pitched deep but thin. This was obviously the congressman.

"Delighted to meet you, Dick," said Parker.

There followed the silence of shaking hands.

"Let's go inside," said the first voice, Davis. By its assurance, I took a guess and matched it up with the mug in the sunglasses. I heard a door close inside the office; low sounds followed, but they were not distinguishable as words. I would have to get closer.

Next to the appraiser's office was a darkened door that read "P. Elwood, Dentist. We Use Gas." I extracted a penknife from my jacket, and with the enthusiasm of a Boy Scout, had Elwood's door opened in a matter of seconds.

The door squeaked slightly, opening into a small reception area, bare except for a half-dozen folding chairs and a low metal table covered with magazines. I pushed the door closed, but kept the lights off. There was noise coming from the appraiser's office, but still no conversation. I followed the battered linoleum down a short hallway to Dr. Elwood's dental chambers. The door was open. It was a small glum office, the final resting place for a dental career that probably began with a correspondence course. The shelves were lined with old instruments, many of which looked unused, some in their original boxes. Moldings of bridgework smiled at me like the glee club of a graveyard.

I seated myself in the motorized chair reserved for patients; the sink next to it was so deeply stained that I figured Elwood crapped in it during office hours. He was either the least successful dentist in Los Angeles or the office was some kind of a front. But it had one towering thing going for it: through a common wall you could hear every word uttered in the adjacent office.

"I think we're all agreed," Davis was saying, "on the need for utmost confidentiality on this. Whatever we say here, stays here. That should be our guiding principle: say here, stays here."

"Absolutely," said Parker. "But I'd like to emphasize that I can only speak for myself here; you realize that I can't speak for the entire industry."

"Of course," replied Davis. "Congressman, you have a few comments?"

A congressional throat was cleared. "Thank you, Mr. Davis," Nixon began. "First of all, I'd like Mr. Parker to know that the House Committee on Un-American Activities deeply appreciates the effort he is making to help us crack the hard shell of Communist activity in our great movie industry." It sounded like he was reading from a sheet. "Without the patriotic help of industry leaders, our investigation is doomed to fruitlessness."

"I appreciate that, Mr. Congressman," Parker said, after a moment's awkward silence. "I'm sure that you'll find that we in the movie business are as eager as you are to clean up. The picture business, first and foremost, is an American business." He paused and fumbled for words. "This investigation, though, when do you foresee it going public?"

"You mean public hearings?" asked the congressman.

"That's right."

"No date has been set as far as I know," Nixon said. "Mr. Davis, do you know?"

"The committee wants to gauge the extent of the subversion before opening up into the public sphere," said Davis. "We don't intend to go on a fishing expedition. When we undertake actual hearings, Dick Nixon and the other great members of the committee will be prepared to name names."

"Of course," said Parker. He sounded very unhappy.

"But we don't want a lot of indiscriminate name-calling, do we?"

"There won't be any indiscriminate name-calling, Mr. Parker," said Nixon, in a stern, hand-on-the-Bible voice. "I can assure you of that. You have my word that this is going to be a sober, responsible investigation of the extent to which the Red shadow has fallen over Hollywood."

Another uneasy silence followed.

"I think Mr. Parker would like to know why we wanted to see him today," said Davis.

"As soon as you called," said Parker. "I cleared the deck of appointments."

"Don't think we don't know and fully appreciate that," Davis replied. "But you're a busy man, so let's get on with it. We're frankly concerned, Johnny, about this Adrian business. Now we all know that Walter Adrian was on our preliminary list as a fully identifiable, card-carrying Communist, dedicated to the goals of the Party. As you and I discussed last week, his continued employment might be of great embarrassment to Warner Brothers."

"That's correct," stammered Parker. "But as I told you, there were no grounds for dismissal and the writers have a very strong union. The only way to handle the situation was to make the contract negotiations with Adrian as difficult as possible. We were proceeding along that route when, of course, the suicide . . ."

"We have information at our disposal," Davis interrupted, his voice dull and relentless, "FBI information on the Adrian death."

"FBI?" Parker's voice was a virtual canary chirp. I got out of the dentist's chair and moved to a stool by the wall, placing my ear flush to it.

"There is information to indicate that Walter Adrian was murdered," Davis continued. "That is why we had to see you today."

"This is FBI information," Nixon repeated, coming

down hard on the magical initials. These guys kept saying "FBI information" as if it were a voodoo incantation.

"There's evidence of murder?" asked Parker.

"Not court evidence, but strong circumstantial evidence, apparently. The congressman and I haven't seen it, actually," Davis went on, "but the source is unimpeachable. What we are telling you, of course, is top secret. It is imperative that no one learn Adrian was murdered or even that there is suspicion of murder."

Parker said something like "of course." He did not say that a private detective had been shot at the previous afternoon and that said detective also suspected foul play. The executive was obviously playing his own game and the case was getting more muddled by the second.

"It's not that we don't have complete confidence in you, John," Davis said with utmost sincerity. "But this is very explosive stuff. Not a word."

Nixon got into the act.

"Let me say, in fact, that we have *great* confidence in your integrity and candor. But this is a matter involving grave matters of national security," the congressman said, emphasizing "grave." "You see, the FBI information indicates that Adrian was murdered on orders direct from Moscow. The word was out in the Red police underground that Adrian would step forward and pass on critical information to the House Committee, information concerning the operation of the Communist Party in Hollywood, and in show business in general."

"Communist espionage, you see," Davis added, "is well aware of the imminence of the investigation."

"Communists murdering writers?" Parker's tone approached shell shock.

"You can see what chaos would follow if this information were made public," said Davis.

"Certainly," the executive mumbled. "Was Adrian about to contact you? Is that a fact?"

"The great tragedy of the Walter Adrian affair," Nixon intoned, "is that we will never know. To be perfectly candid, Mr. Parker, Adrian had not yet come to us, or given any signals that he would. I would imagine that a dedicated, hardcore Communist would have to go through a great deal of painful soul-searching before reaching such a momentous decision." This kid Nixon sounded like a radio preacher. And I, for one, couldn't figure Walter running to the law to tell them which of his friends belonged to the Party. It didn't sound like him, it didn't wash. Yet as hokey and outrageous as it was to assume that Walter had been bumped off on orders from some drab-suited Stalinist torpedo, it bothered me. It bothered me because there was something nuts and out of focus about this whole case, something that no one was talking about, not Walter to me in New York, nor Walter's friends at his home. There were loose ends of fear and mistrust that Nixon's and Davis' cockamaymie theory could conceivably explain. Maybe Walter *was* scared enough to talk, maybe someone *did* find out and finish him off, if not by Kremlin orders then by personal motivation. Nothing made a great deal of sense in the matter: the Red knock-off theory was no more implausible than Walter swinging on the back lot, or the cops getting an FBI report on my pinko record, or my sitting in a shabby dentist's office eavesdropping on a Warner Brothers executive and a U.S. Congressman.

"You can see why no one must hear of this," said Davis, "and why we must get to the roots of this operation before too long."

"The plain fact is," the congressman said smoothly, "that the way the Communists enforce discipline—using Adrian's death as an example—it'll soon be impossible for us to get the information we need."

"I see," Parker babbled. "Naturally. We'll do all we can. Within the limit of the law, of course; we have to be subtle."

"Subtlety," announced Davis, "is of the essence. That's our watchword."

"Are the L.A. police being brought in on this?" asked Parker.

The room fell silent.

"Not unless it's an absolute necessity," Davis finally said. "Too many boneheads in the department. They could blow this thing wide open."

"That's what I would think," the executive concurred.

"Now, let's not go overboard on this," Nixon interjected. "The Los Angeles Police Department contains some of the finest men in the country: dedicated, patriotic Americans. All Mr. Davis is saying is that this is one of those cases where too many cooks would spoil the broth."

"Exactly, Dick. That's how I see it," Davis reassured him. "So, Johnny, to wrap this up in a neat package, we need your fullest cooperation at the quickest possible speed, in getting us names and witnesses. We don't want a wave of murders, so we've got to smash this thing before it gets out of control."

"I understand."

"And of course," said Davis, "everything to be done in as circumspect and unobtrusive a manner as possible."

"Rest assured . . ." the Warners executive began to say, but never finished. The other men arose with much scraping of chairs on the floor.

"I think we should leave first, Dick," Davis told the congressman.

"Fine," he replied. "I hope Mr. Parker didn't find this a too out-of-the-way location. I know how busy he must be at the studio."

"No problem," Parker said manfully.

"But we must meet under these kinds of conditions," Nixon continued, "to outwit a very shrewd and determined enemy. The only way to defeat deviousness and guile is to show a little deviousness and guile yourself. That's what the

American people don't understand yet. They still think the Russians are our friends, they still think we're fighting the Germans together."

"Check," Davis concurred.

"But we're not," Nixon went on.

"That's right, we're not," Parker said, somewhat half-heartedly, I thought. I got the impression that Nixon was standing a half-inch from Parker, breathing a civics lesson into his face.

"No, we're fighting an enemy skilled beyond our imagination in the arts of subversion and espionage," Nixon said urgently. "Who would have thought this great movie industry of ours would be honeycombed with men and women whose first allegiance was to Moscow."

"As much of a shock to me, sir . . ." Parker attempted to say.

"So we've got to fight this fight," Nixon was unrelenting, "in places like this. Lonely, drab places. Meeting in secret, in hiding. Like a war. Because that's what this is, a war."

"Dick, we've got to go," Davis said.

Final salutations were exchanged, then the two men left the inner office and walked out into the hall. I hustled back to Elwood's reception room and listened at the door. There was nothing to hear but two pairs of footsteps echoing down the hall. They paused, then exited via the stairs. I waited. Five minutes later, Parker took his leave, locking the office and walking briskly to the elevator. I heard the elevator doors open and close, then opened Elwood's door a crack and saw that the hall was empty. I closed up the office and raced for the stairs. The elevator was at three and descending. I flew down the stairs, through the lobby, and out into the street, turning the corner just as Parker emerged, blinking into the sunshine. He affixed sunglasses to his skull and disappeared inside the Rolls. I opened up my Chrysler and slid way down in the seat. The Rolls started up and moved out, taking a left on Third. I waited a beat and then resumed my pursuit of Johnny Parker. It was clear to me that all the action was flowing his way.

I was not mistaken.

We drove all the way back to Beverly Hills, a dull forty-minute trek. I yawned at lights and drummed my fingers on the dash. Traffic got extremely light as we entered Beverly Hills and I had to lay way back. Unless Parker was unconscious he was bound to notice the omnipresence of the black Chrysler.

Parker turned onto Rodeo Drive and pulled into the circular driveway of a white mansion. I stopped my car on Gregory and watched. Parker got out of the Rolls, holding his keys, and unlocked the ten-foot-high door of what I presumed to be his house. I sat and waited, undisturbed and undistracted. Gregory was a typically quiet Beverly Hills street, bearing no signs of human habitation: no stores, no people, no children scampering wildly on the sidewalks. There weren't even sidewalks. Just perfectly green and trimmed lawns, fronting gigantic homes that seemed to be lived in by automobiles. Gregory Street was soundless, except for birdsong and distant traffic.

And except for the white Cadillac convertible that suddenly sped past me, doing a conspicuous sixty miles per hour.

The Caddy hurtled down the street, turned left, and whipped around Parker's driveway, screeching to a stop bare inches behind the majestic Rolls. The driver of the Caddy jumped out and ran up to Parker's door. He leaned on the bell. The chimes could be faintly heard from where I sat. I removed a small but powerful pair of binoculars from my pocket and observed Parker's frantic visitor, pushing the bell over and over, holding a manila envelope in his hand.

It was Dale Carpenter, the cowboy actor.

The door opened and Parker expressed evident surprise

and consternation. He recovered and shook the actor's hand, quickly guiding him into the house. Before closing the door behind them, Parker looked around in the classic, sickly manner of one fearful of observation. He *was* being watched. And so, in turn, was the watcher being watched.

I got out of my car and headed for Parker's house. It was a clumsy, witless play, but I didn't see any alternative, not if I wanted to remain even in remote touch with this case. I knew far too little to allow Carpenter to visit Parker, and spend that time half a block away snoozing in my car. It was worth the risk to get closer.

Then again, it wasn't worth the risk at all. The rest is dream. As I closed the car door, a large and moist hand clapped itself over my mouth and I heard a sharp intake of breath behind me. I turned to look, but as I did an opera house fell on my head. Time stretched wet and warm. Black waves pounded somewhere. I gazed down at my feet, but they were miles beneath me. I floated down, spinning toward my shoes very slowly, like a parachutist caught in a crosswind, descending at a snowflake's pace. I couldn't see my feet, then they flashed into view again, turning orange. The thought occurred to a part of me that I hadn't seen the man who had just smashed my skull, but it took much too long to think it all the way through, and as I neared the end of the thought, my shoes were racing up to meet me, and there was only time to crash.

8

A sea wind blew the closed blinds out and back, smacking against the open window. The room was dim and evening was settling into the ocean outside; gulls screeched and swooped to the rhythms of the dinner bell. Skimming the waters, I thought, adjusting their wings ever so slightly, fading orange sunset reflected on their bellies. Very free and beautiful. Very much unlike myself, a bald man bound hand and foot to a lumpy, fetid mattress.

My waking came in drugged stages. Not only had I been skulled, but a beaker of mind-numbing chemicals had been indiscriminately added to the LeVine bloodstream. Miraculously, I had come to once or twice, leaden and half-witted with sedation. The air was moist and my clothes soaked; if I'd had any hair, it would have been matted. Instead, water streamed down my face.

The first two times my eyes opened, I was flailing through a legless panic of back-alley flight. The waking was just another layer of marbled, patchy sleep. I had nothing to grasp onto and spiraled back downward to a series of blurred Technicolor vignettes: a hardware store set on the banks of the Amazon, pursuit by long-dead relatives, and an abrupt, disquieting meeting with my very own self, aged white and wandering pitifully through an empty lot in Corona, Queens. A confused fight with a Bungalow Bar man ensued, Walter Adrian coming to my aid. Night fell instantly, the sky filling with the sad dim stars of a moonlit corner in a comic strip.

The third time my lids opened, I swam closer to the surface of consciousness, experiencing sea sounds. I breathed deeply, felt no sensation in my arms or legs, and attempted to construct something in the nature of a thought about that fact, but my brain cells shorted out and I sank to the bottom once again. I was home in Sunnyside, somehow trapped beneath my living room couch. Hip-booted men stalked the house looking for me. They opened the oven door.

The fourth time I awoke nearly for keeps, struggling into the tangible world with considerable effort, like someone climbing a flight of iced-over stairs. My eyes opened and I could not tell if the room was dark or if my vision had been impaired. I had no more sense of time or place than a goldfish.

A bare bulb dangled by a cord above my bed. I thought the bulb was switched off, then perceived that it generated a nimbus of light. Slow and dim-witted reflection followed: how does a juiceless bulb give off light? It doesn't, I concluded. It can't. That problem resolved and instantly forgotten, a cigarette hole in my mind, I turned my full attention to the window. Behind the banging blinds there appeared to be a beach. It smelled and sounded like a beach, and it was evening, given over to sandpipers and solitary walkers. I wanted to take a walk.

But my ability to walk was seriously limited by the fact that my arms were spread-eagled and roped clumsily to the bedsprings, and my feet bound with clothesline. When I made the logical move to stretch and yawn upon what I believed to be waking, I almost snapped my backbone in two. This frightened me terribly. Unless you've been tied down in such a fashion, you cannot imagine the crawly sensation of vulnerability, the anxiety of being as passive, as *available,* as an open-faced sandwich or a stiff on a slab. My mind wasn't yet supple enough to determine why and how I had gotten into such a miserable posture. I tried to float my brain from my skull like a helium balloon, but the attempt was stillborn; it was all I could do to remember my name.

So I lay there sweating, as stupidly afraid as a child locked in nighttime combat with talking closets and fiendish chests of drawers. I awaited the arrival of white-gowned Dr. Frankenstein, wheeling in a rolling cart glistening with syringes and retorts and test tubes all abubble. Electrodes would be attached to my head; sizzling electrical currents, zigzags of horrific lightning, and the job would be done. I would obey any command. I would walk into the sea.

Fifth time down, but the submergence seemed shorter, lighter, than my previous dips and tailspins. When I awoke, pale evening light still filtered through the blinds and voices shouted from the beach. I was wetter than ever, but my edge had returned; the chemicals seemed to have been flushed from my pores and I no longer feared, or even considered, the bogeyman. Jack was back, faster than his captors had guessed, if the sloppiness of the rope-work on my hands was any tip-off. If you want to keep a six-foot, two hundred-pound man out for half a day, you have to drug him nearly to death. Someone had not wanted to take that risk. Looking back, I don't really understand why not.

It took over an hour of ceaseless rubbing and tugging to free my right hand. I had to perform the task silently, and stopped every time I heard warning noises outside the door. There was a radio emitting soft, dull sounds that might have been music, punctuated by an occasional cough and the regular splashing of liquor into a glass. Cigarette smoke wafted into my room. I completed the picture: a bored and cranky thug playing solitaire and getting plastered, the cards lined up on a metal kitchen table, right next to an oiled gun. The picture encouraged me; if I was to get out of here, it would be a good deal easier to slip past one man than two, and a great deal easier if the one man had dulled his reflexes through boredom and whiskey. That's how I figured it. I was wrong, of course, but that's nothing new.

I finally got the rope sufficiently loosened to withdraw my right hand, then rolled over quietly and undid the left. When I leaned forward ever so slightly, in an effort to reach my feet, my brains slid down to my stomach and I had to lie back down again, or faint from dizziness, sick chills, and intestinal revolution. There I lay, coated with perspiration, listening to the waves, the gulls, and the radio. I noticed that the window, while slightly open, was barred, and wondered if passersby were not struck by the presence of bars on a beach house.

A chair scraped against linoleum and I heard the solitaire player get up. I twined the rope around my right hand, the hand that faced the door, and shut my eyes. A key was inserted, somewhat clumsily, and the door swung open. I breathed heavily, spread-eagled on the bed and lost to the free world. A man entered the room and chuckled.

"How's the weather down there?" he asked in a husky voice.

He laughed again. I felt his attention for a few more seconds, then he left the room and relocked the door.

"Out like a dead bulb," he said outside. The grunt he received in reply came as a shock. Two men. They had been as silent as one. The lack of chatter meant that they were either complete strangers or old friends, long past words. Which meant, in turn, that I had no clue as to whether the two men could be played off against each other.

I leaned forward again, into a shimmering swell of nausea, and undid my feet, leaving the cord wrapped loosely about the ankles.

"When's he coming back, he say definite?" a voice asked.

"Late. Two or three."

"Then we take the dick right out?"

"About ten, twelve miles out."

"And a mile deep."

They shared a good laugh over that one. I failed to see the humor in it. The prospect of being left as a kosher snack for a slew of sharks was unimaginably grim, but my mind was still too deadened to appreciate the full horror of it. The threat of getting tossed to fish with big teeth was so outside my experience, so wildly melodramatic, that I couldn't work up a man-sized scream. Instead, I concentrated on finer, detective-school details, like getting the hell out of this house on the beach. It was early evening and "he" wasn't returning until the early A.M., leaving me a great deal of leeway.

I reached over and felt through my jacket, which was draped hunchbacked over a chair. The gun, of course, had vanished, but my binoculars remained. I took them out and gripped them tightly in my right hand, then resumed my snoring posture on the mattress. I closed my eyes and awaited the next bed check.

An hour or so passed. It was now very nearly dark outside. The ocean surf was beating harder, more ominously on the shore. I might have dozed a bit, I can't remember anymore. But I heard the chair scrape against the floor again, then a key bumped around the lock before getting accurately inserted. I guessed that the waiting had gotten to my night nurse; he had been drinkng way too much.

The door opened and closed, and a cloud of alcoholic breath blew my way. I commenced mumbling.

"How's the weather down there?" he asked as before.

"Cunt . . . tits," I murmured, twisting my shoulders and hips as best I could.

There was no reply, just a further density in the air as bourbon fumes proceeded the lowering of his head. Attentive silence hung suspended above my face.

"Big tits," I gargled thickly, then turned my head slightly. I began to snore.

"Goddamn," he said softly. He shook my head, trying to coax out some more wet dreaming.

"C'mon," I growled, suddenly brutal and bear-like. "Abbaba. Put it in your mmmn."

"What?" he said. "Your what?"

I heard a high thin voice from the next room.

"You talking to me, Mex?"

My avid listener raised his head and stepped to the door, stumbling as he went. "The dick's talking dirty to himself," he called through the door. "Wanna hear?"

"No," the man shouted back. "Fight's coming on. If you're staying in there, shut the fuckin door."

The door closed. I smelled Mex's fiery breath, felt increased body heat, as his face neared mine.

"Sabbalar . . . fuh. Come on, baby," I pleaded. "My cah . . . cah."

"What?" Mex whispered urgently. I had him.

"Take it in your hand," I said softly, smiling in my sleep. "Now squeeze it. Squeeeeze it."

I groaned and Mex groaned with me.

"Christ," he said with difficulty. "I could use some of that."

"Now, open your mouth," I said, cutting my volume. "No, wider. That's it. That's it." I lowered my voice to an indecipherable mumble. The last audible word I issued forth was "tongue."

Mex put his ear to my mouth like an anxious doctor checking for signs of life. At which point I successfully whipped my right hand around and sapped him with the binoculars. He fell in a heap on top of me, as much victimized by drink as by the blow.

I rolled Mex over and off me, arranging him neatly on the bed, tying his hands to the bedsprings and binding his ankles with the rope I had kicked from mine. Then I arose, slowly and with head pounding, and crept behind the door, binoculars in hand. The radio in the next room was tuned to a prizefight; introductions from the ring were in progress.

"Hey, Mex," the man called. "Fight's about to start."

I tensed and gripped the binoculars tightly in my fist.

"Mex!" he repeated, more loudly. "The fight!"

Mex wasn't receiving messages, and a quizzical silence filled the next room. The other man turned the volume down on the radio, then pushed his chair back and stepped to the door. I held myself rigid against the wall, my knees knocking from fatigue, weakness, and the aftermath of a chemical riot in my system.

"Mex?" he said softly through the door. He was right outside now, standing quietly and trying to assess the situation, aware with a thug's logic that something had gone a little screwy. I didn't know whether he'd tiptoe in or launch a full siege, gun drawn. Either way, I had the lie on him.

The door opened. Saying "I told you to quit juicing," the man entered the room cautiously, a revolver in his paw. I brought the binoculars down on his head the second it appeared through the door. It was a fine shot and the man, thick-necked and attired in corduroy pants and a fisherman's sweater, fell down heavily. So did I. My knees gave way and I went to the floor, breathing rapidly and with effort, coughing up and swallowing some bile.

It took a few minutes for me to gather enough strength to stand up again. I walked over to the bed and undid one of Mex's hands, giving me enough rope to tie his friend's arms together above the elbow. If you do it tightly enough, the circulation gets cut to zero and the victim awakes with arms of stone. I did the same for Mex and then bid them both adieu.

I left the bedroom. Outside was a small kitchen, containing a stove, a refrigerator, and a tattered, ruined linoleum floor. An Emerson was perched on the white metal kitchen table. I turned up the volume just as a fighter named Morales was getting knocked on his ass in San

Diego. I didn't much care. I found my gun resting on a rose-decaled breadbox and made very sure that it was still loaded. Then I dropped it into my jacket pocket and exited from the house through a screen door. I had no idea of where I was but a good idea of where I wanted to be. Back home with Helen Adrian.

I closed the screen door softly behind me and emerged into the cool, damp evening air. Crickets were conversing steadily, and two hundred feet to my immediate right, the Pacific surf rumbled and broke upon the shore. I breathed deeply, a lost and unhappy man, my mind still clouded over with drug-induced mysteries. When you awake from a nightmare, the discomfort nags at you for hours afterward, undigested. If the nightmare has come from the tip of a needle, the spooks hang around for days and weeks; they roll out from under the carpet at peculiar, disorienting intervals. They shake tambourines and roll their eyes. You try to recall making their acquaintance.

I stood outside the door for a very long moment, acclimating myself to the surroundings. I was on a concrete path next to the side entrance of a back apartment located in a three-story, brown-shingled Cape Cod saltbox home, the last house on a residential street that ended in sand and scrub brush. There was a fire-scorched lot next door, and a half-dozen low-slung beach houses quite a distance beyond that. Lights were on in those houses, and music was playing. I didn't know where the hell I was but I did know that I should be getting away from the saltbox house, so I started down the road, passing a sea-rusted street sign that informed me I was hurrying down Pacific Way.

Pacific Way followed the coastline for a few hundred yards, then dropped down and to the east. I stopped and gaped at one of the lit beach houses, a wooden structure of recent design, with the look of a gull alighting on the sand. Through a window I observed two young couples seated around a dinner table, drinking red wine from goblets and laughing uproariously. I stared at the scene with the bewildered awe of a child come downstairs to his parents' noisy party. After rejecting a notion to knock on their door and ask exactly where I was, I left Pacific Way as quickly as possible to hunt down a public phone.

Two hundred yards down the road and the ocean disappeared from view. I was sorry to see it go. The road was dark and untrafficked, bordered by dense, wild foliage. After a quarter-mile, I came to a small garage and filling station. The boy on duty was spread out beneath a Pontiac that dated from the Ming Dynasty. A light rain began to fall. I coughed to announce myself and he came squirming out from under, a husky kid in his late teens.

He gazed at me from the ground, still on his back, his blond hair caked with oil and dust.

"Sir?" he asked.

"I need a phone. You got one?"

"We got one, but it's on the fritz. Car break down?"

"Yeah, ways up the road."

"Want me to bring it in for you?"

I hemmed, I hawed, and finally assembled some clever excuse like I was short of cash and wanted to call the wife. She had the money, you see, and the garage we usually use. . . . Luckily, the boy wasn't listening.

"Up to you, Mister," he said indifferently, disappearing beneath the Pontiac. "You want a phone, there's one at Vince's restaurant."

"Where's that?"

Only his blond, dusty hair was visible.

"Mile and a half," he said.

The mile and a half took about forty minutes. I can walk a good deal faster than that, but the drugs had left me with the legs of a hippo. I lumbered down the road, panting and sweating, sitting down at regular intervals on boulders or chopped-down sections of weed, confused, afraid, and—another echo of my chemical experience—

paranoid. In that forty minutes, I must have looked behind me two dozen times, and heard the approach of phantom autos a dozen more. When really anxious, I tried running, but run turned to lope turned to walk in a matter of seconds. I was in no kind of shape at all.

So I was very happy to see Vince's loom in the distance, a glow of red neon backed by a strangely shapeless mountain, one that seemed to shift like a cloud, its boulders mere smoke. I picked up my step, but seemed to make no headway; if anything, the restaurant appeared to recede, its sheltering mountain loosed from its moorings, gliding up and back. A madman's sweating panic ensued and I attempted once again to run. My chest grew tight and a pounding commenced at the back of my head. I stumbled and fell. A long roundhouse curve of wind blew past, clearing out a field of fog. The lights of the restaurant grew bright, the mountain became solid and familiar. I continued to sit in the road, an idiot's grin pasted to my face, gawking like Dorothy from Kansas at the sight of Oz.

I arose with dignity and dusted my pants. Perspective returned: I was hungry and wanted to eat, and I was anxious to call Helen Adrian, for a rush of reasons I lacked the keen wit to sort out and identify. I told myself that I wanted to reassure the lady, but you don't need a psychiatrist's shingle to figure out that it was LeVine himself who needed the reassurance.

Vince's restaurant was no mirage. It was a serene and squat concrete blockhouse, flat-roofed and adorned by a classy red neon sign that spelled Vince's name in fiery script. Inside it was just a joint. It had a short black counter lined by a half-dozen stools, and a half-dozen tables, one of them occupied by a family. It had all that, plus a pervasive and not unpleasant odor of garlic. There was a phone mounted on the wall next to a jukebox; I went to it immediately, scrounging through my pockets for a nickel.

An operator intercepted the call and informed me I'd have to come up with another nickel. I asked her why and she explained that a call from the Santa Monica district to Los Angeles required two nickels, not one. Relieved to know where I was, I obligingly coughed up another five cents.

Helen answered. As calmly as I could—to avoid panic on her end—I explained myself. The lady didn't panic, of course, she never did; she told me that she'd leave at once and come retrieve me. I relayed, as best I could, the precise location of Vince's.

"I know the place. Walter and I stopped there once or twice. It has something of a local reputation. Get the canneloni."

"How are you doing?" I asked.

"I'm a little numb, but not too bad, all things considered. It's been a long day. I had just now begun to worry about you."

"Can you drive?"

"Sure," she said. "No problem."

"You positive?"

"Absolutely. Say listen, how did the famous detective wind up at Vince's without his car?"

"There's an amusing story in that. Come get me before they do, know what I mean?"

"Know what you mean," she repeated, and hung up. She might have smacked a kiss into the receiver, but I wouldn't swear to it.

I wandered over to the counter and lowered my prize rump onto a stool. A handsome, black-haired man with a bold Roman nose and unhappy eyes greeted me. His sports shirt and brown poplin slacks were immaculate, despite the bubbling pots of tomato sauce.

"You Vince?"

He nodded silently, whipping a small white pad and a pen from his shirt pocket.

"I'd like some canneloni," I told him, "and a small salad." He nodded and scribbled. "Plenty of bread, coffee," he continued to nod, "and a little information." Vince stopped nodding. He tore my order off the pad, pressed his arms against the counter, and leaned forward.

"What kind of information?" he asked in a mellow baritone suggestive of acting lessons.

"Nothing fancy," I told him, "and I could use that coffee right now."

Vince picked a glass percolator off a double burner and filled up a cup, never taking his eyes off me. I wondered if a scarlet letter or a bluish bulge was radiating from my forehead. My fingers found no facial swelling but did feel out a nice lump, protruding from the base of my skull like the beginnings of another head.

"Take a fall?" asked Vince.

I shook my head and invented a chuckle.

"My nephew. He thinks he's Hugh Casey. Bounced a fastball off me last weekend. Hurt like hell."

Vince nodded sympathetically.

"Those things really smart. Let me put your canneloni in."

He vanished into a small kitchen, while I sipped his excellent coffee. I closed my eyes and wished I were in bed.

Vince returned, wiping his hands on a towel.

"So what did you want to know?" he asked.

"Well, I was out by Pacific Way before. I'm from the East, as you might've guessed."

"It was easy." Vince grinned and revealed a set of capped choppers every bit as perfect as Dick Powell's.

"Sure, I'm a dead giveaway," I said amiably. "Anyhow, that Pacific Way caught my fancy and I've been thinking of moving out here. You know if anything's for sale?"

"On Pacific?"

"Right."

"Not that I know of." He picked a toothpick out of a small cut-glass bowl and inserted the pick next to an incisor. He waggled it contemplatively, pleased to be discussing real estate.

"Tell you the one I'm thinking of, Vince," I said, warming to the task, the coffee beginning to awake my comatose brain cells. "There's a burned-out lot, and next to it is a sweet old saltbox, three stories. Rundown, but nothing a few bucks couldn't set right. Looked deserted to me."

Vince nodded. "I know the one you're thinking of, but it's not up for grabs. Lady named Brownell owned it. Widow, no kids. She died and a nephew of hers got it. He's not around much, but I haven't heard that he's selling."

"You know him if you saw him?"

"Who?"

"The nephew."

He shrugged. A few questions like that and anybody working a Tenth Avenue hash house would have asked to see the shingle. But this was the Golden West, and Vince was no more suspicious of me than he was of his pasta.

"Nope," he concluded, taking his arms from the counter, "I could ask around for you, but I'm pretty sure he's not selling. I'll get your dinner."

The canneloni was delicious. The salad was fresh, the dressing homemade and spiced with onion. Served with a loaf of hot Italian bread and a tub of butter, the meal preserved my sanity until Helen Adrian arrived.

She was wearing a raincoat over a rumpled blue sweater and black slacks. Vince blinked a few times when she walked in the door; it was around eight-thirty and we were the only people in the joint.

"I know you," said Vince. "You've eaten here."

"That's right," Mrs. Adrian told him, smiling politely. She sat down on the stool next to mine and shook out her hair. "Starting to rain. Coffee, Vince."

Vince pushed a cup in front of her and filled it up. She swiveled around on her stool and faced me. She smiled.

"And here we are," she said, peering at my skull. Her hand touched my lump, as lightly as a sudden breeze. "What's that?"

"A bump."

"Oh really?" She sounded amused and leaned toward me, smelling of wet wool. "In the line of duty?"

"That's right."

A strand of damp red hair fell across her left eye as she lowered her head to sip some coffee. She smoothed it away with her ring finger. The angle of her head, the lips pursed on the rim of the cup, her smooth cheek, the cozy, dense smell of wool; all of that, plus my fragile state of mind, sent me right off the tracks for her.

She caught me staring at her. "You're smiling," she said.

"I'm happy."

Vince backed away from the counter, fearful of eavesdropping, and strolled into the kitchen. Mrs. Adrian and I sat hunched over our coffee cups, knees almost touching; a peculiar, pleasing moment.

"We better blow," I told her.

"Are there really people after you?"

"They should still be out of commission, but you can't ever be sure." I got worried as I said the words. "I'd really like to get out of here."

Mrs. Adrian picked up on my apprehension.

"Fine with me."

I called for Vince and he walked out of the kitchen. I paid him. He said he'd keep his eyes peeled for any houses opening up on Pacific. I thanked him, promised to stay in touch. Mrs. Adrian and I went outside; it was still raining. Her white Olds was parked right outside the door. We got in and headed out onto the dark two-lane road. Mrs. Adrian brought the car right up to sixty-five. I winced but kept a discreet silence.

"What was that all about?" she asked. "About the house."

"I told him I was interested in real estate on Pacific

Way, in order to find out about this house I found myself in a couple of hours ago."

"What do you mean, 'found yourself'?"

"I mean 'found myself' in the sense of coming to after being smashed in the head on a Beverly Hills street, getting drugged to imbecility and then tied down, hand and foot, to an old bed. That's what 'found myself' refers to. And I wish you'd watch the road."

She watched me instead.

"Somebody did that to you?"

"Some bodies. I'd guess it was the same party responsible for killing Walter and for the shots at me on the Western Street."

"Oh Christ." Mrs. Adrian patted my hand. "You have to be careful, Jack."

"I'm just lucky I didn't get killed right off the bat. Must have been a foul-up."

"Well, you can't kill someone in broad daylight in Beverly Hills," she said analytically. "Or in Santa Monica, for that matter." She raised a thin eyebrow. "How did you get out of that house on Pacific?"

I spent the rest of the trip to Beverly Hills describing my painful odyssey after the funeral. Mrs. Adrian bit her lip in tension, oohed and aahed, and almost cheered at the happy ending. She was a terrific audience.

"The upshot is that if he had arrived earlier, you would have been killed," she said when I had finished.

"They overestimated the strength of the drugs or underestimated my bearish constitution."

The lady smiled.

"You're such a tough guy."

"I am tough," I pretended to protest, realizing instantly that we had begun to play a lovers' game, the mock argument. The playfulness was followed by an uncertain silence in the car. Mrs. Adrian's smile stayed fixed, then faded; she held her eyes to the road and finally turned on the wipers as the rain quickened. I felt a chill.

"I missed you today," she said after a while.

I settled back in my seat, leaning my head against a custom-made rest.

"The house was filled with people after the funeral," she continued, "talking and eating, arguing. I went upstairs and cried for a while. That's when I missed you. You were the only person I wanted to talk to."

"I'm a good listener," I told her. "It goes with the profession."

"You're a good listener and a good person, Jack. An un-neurotic and decent man."

"I'm not so sure about the neurotic part," I said, "but it's nice to hear."

We pulled onto Gregory Street and stopped in back of the Chrysler, which was standing there as if nothing had happened.

"I'll follow you," I told Mrs. Adrian.

"You still have the keys?"

I fished through my pockets, found the keys and displayed them.

"Fine," she said. "I'll drive slowly."

The rain had thinned out again, but the air inside the Olds smelled of the damp.

"Hurry up," said Helen Adrian, her voice turning soft and uncertain.

I didn't hurry up. Mrs. Adrian tilted her head and I bent forward and kissed her. Nothing spectacular; the kiss was in the nature of an understanding.

She straightened up and squeezed my hand.

"C'mon, Jack," she said more briskly. "Let's go."

I got out of the car and walked over to the Chrysler. Mrs. Adrian brought the Olds beside me as I started up, then she pulled down Gregory Street and I dutifully followed, suddenly aware that I was terribly tired.

We reached the Adrian house in about twenty minutes. Mrs. Adrian put the Olds in the garage, then walked across the broad wet lawn. The rain was visible against the porch light as she hurriedly opened the door and went inside. I sat in the Chrysler for a moment, wondering if the lady were angry at me, or at herself. Or angry at all. Under the circumstances, I was prepared to understand and accept any mood or frame of mind; I was ready for hurled china-ware, weeping, bitter imprecations. I had, perhaps, taken advantage of her vulnerability. But I was pretty vulnerable myself, detective license or not. I began thinking that I was making a large to-do out of very little and got out of the car.

When I walked through the open door she was standing in the foyer, staring at me quizzically, her hands dug deep into the pockets of her wet raincoat.

"Hold me, Jack," she said, and I did so, wrapping my arms around her strong back. She kept her hands in her pockets and rested her head on my shoulder.

"A long day," she said quietly. "You must be exhausted."

"You, too."

"Nobody smacked me on the head." Mrs. Adrian lifted her head and put her hands on my shoulders. A long finger stroked my ear. "It's the attention that exhausted me, know what I mean?"

I nodded.

"All that attention," she repeated. "It can drive you nuts." She dropped her hands and took a step back. "Why don't you draw yourself a bath and I'll bring you some cognac, okay?"

"Sounds terrific."

A rich and tired smile tightened her eyes into small, contented points of green.

"Good. Jacket?"

She took my sports jacket and hung it up with her rain-coat, then tossed her hair and headed for the living room. I stood by the stairs and watched her walk. She knew it, and turned to face me.

"Go take your bath, Jack." She smiled. "Step on it."

I kicked off my shoes and climbed the stairs, a fat bald child on the night before Christmas.

Her knock surprised me. I was half-asleep in the tub, lulled to dreaming by the scalding water I had drawn.

"Cognac girl," she announced.

I drew the curtain, leaving only my head visible, and beckoned her in. Mrs. Adrian entered carrying a silver tray with two large snifters of brandy. She placed the tray on the closed toilet.

"This is how they do it in the best restaurants," she said.

I yawned.

"Were you asleep?" she asked, placing a snifter into my wet grasp.

"I'm at the point where I don't know if I'm awake or asleep. Are you really in here?"

Mrs. Adrian sat down on the edge of the tub.

"It's me and you know it. So modest; I heard the curtain closing."

"I didn't want you to see the little tugboats."

She chuckled deeply, a little wickedly.

"Such a card," she said. "Mr. New Yorker."

I sipped some cognac and leaned my head against the white enamel, resting the stem of the snifter upon my submerged chest. My muscles were relaxing, loosening; peace suffused my limbs and nerves.

My eyes closed again, briefly; I caught a short warm gust of sleep.

When my eyes opened, Mrs. Adrian was standing and pulling off her sweater. She reached behind her and unsnapped her brassiere, and caught my stunned, foolish gaze.

"I thought you were asleep."

"Just for a second."

"Shucks, I wanted to surprise you. Watch out, I'm coming in there with you. Hide the ducks."

I swallowed a bit more cognac, then placed the snifter on the tile floor beside the tub. Mrs. Adrian bent over and stepped out of her slacks and white panties, then pulled the shower curtain open.

"Ta-ta." She hummed her own fanfare, maybe to cover her embarrassment, maybe to cover mine. She had taken her clothes off with such speed and determination as to suggest an act of will. To slow down, to mull it over, might have been to stop altogether.

Mrs. Adrian stuck a tentative toe into the water. "Christ, that's hot."

And there she stood, leg arched in the water, a supportive hand upon the curtain; my September Morn. She had a wonderful body, with the small flaws and soft slackenings of a woman who has lived well, and screw the hourglass curves. She was somewhat high-waisted, with a fairly flat posterior and large, firm breasts. And she could read my mind.

"What do you think?"

"About what?"

"Me. My body."

"Very nice. You coming in?"

She paused for a last moment and then came hurriedly into the long tub, with many oohs and much splashing.

"Aah," she aahed, settling in. There was a rubber pillow on the rim at her end. She rested that startling head upon it.

"And here we are," she announced, "the private eye and the grieving widow."

"That's a hell of a way to look at it."

"I know." Mrs. Adrian took a hefty swig of cognac. "I'm indulging myself. But there is a certain amount of guilt going on down at this end."

"There'd have to be," I offered cautiously.

"Yes," was her equally neutral answer. "When Walter was alive, I felt guilty because I didn't love him. Maybe it'll get worse now."

"I think not; you're a pretty tough girl."

She thought it over.

"You ever married, Jack?"

"For six years."

"And then?"

"Listen, I'm the shamus."

She laughed and splashed some water my way.

"The shamus. What happened to the marriage?"

"Nothing sensational. She wanted a nine-to-five guy and a house full of kids. Now she's got both."

"You bitter?"

"What for?" I heard myself say. "I don't blame her; she just should have known what she was getting into, marrying a private dick."

"Private dick," Mrs. Adrian cooed. "Has a nice ring to it."

We were a pair, all right, doing our little mating dance. I was still apprehensive, half-expecting a monsoon of tears to come blowing my way, but decreasingly so. I was getting used to the fact of our nakedness, getting comfortable with the strangeness of it all.

Some minutes later, I got very comfortable indeed, when Mrs. Adrian's smooth foot burrowed soundlessly into a watery bed beneath my dozing balls. She wiggled her toes. I cackled delightedly. It felt awfully good.

"Hello," she said, her eyes at once innocent and eager. This was some sweet baby.

"Hello," I said. "Can I interest you in a vacuum cleaner?"

She giggled and kept wiggling those educated toes. Then her other foot joined the party. I casually reached over and took another sip of the warming brandy.

"You're so jaded," Mrs. Adrian said, greatly amused. "Such a bore, isn't it?" She lowered her eyes to the water. "Well, lookee here."

A circumcised periscope had surfaced, poking its blind eye through the darkening, glassy currents of the bathwater. It pulsed. It throbbed. We studied it thoughtfully, as if it were a newly arrived guest.

"How lovely," Mrs. Adrian said, and curled her hand around it. I closed my eyes and tipped my hat to the fates.

"I've done my best with it," I said gravely. "Tried to raise it right."

"No more jokes, Jack," she said, both hands on it now, running wet fingers up and back.

I opened my eyes and moved forward in the tub. I raised her legs easily in the water and with the unencumbered grace of true love's dumb luck, I entered the lady in one smooth motion. Like turning a soft lock with a soft key. We lay joined in the water, our hands on each others legs, staring at each other curiously but contentedly, feeling, I think, that this crazy thing was happening simply because it deserved to happen.

We began to rock each other slowly, barely moving, creating small waves that broke over the side of the tub and soaked the floor. Helen closed her eyes, her front tooth biting down softly on a bottom lip drawn into a mellow smile. She made little sounds, clucks of acknowledgment, rising and falling in the shallow water like someone floating in the Rockaway surf. There was at first a weightless, careful quality to our lovemaking, but with the first stirrings of urgency, we left our histories behind and let our bodies take over.

And then we were sea lions, in full, shiny frolic, staying one bristling and barking leap ahead of each other. The leaps grow longer, the arcs higher; we began to lose ourselves in the act. Except for one brief and unsettling moment in which I felt a sudden, peculiar estrangement from the beautiful woman flopping so blissfully about in the water. Who was she? What the hell was I doing? But the moment passed quickly and so did its aftertaste of wonder and doubt—as if losing a familiar, yet indeterminate face in a subway crowd.

117

Our steady rising and yielding grew more intense; our brains flowed sweetly to the very tips of ourselves. The water in the tub had all but vanished, and we thumped in a shallow pool on the white enamel. Helen bit her lip a little harder, flushing pink. "Jack," she said, and then again, "Jack!" She thrashed the remaining water out of the tub, as I took my last leap in a thunderous surf; released, cresting, breaking, and then descending back to the ocean floor, emptied and warm.

And there we lay on the bare enamel, still joined, glistening like a pair of triumphant wrestlers: Jack the Skull and Helen the Red.

"Mmmm," she said. I said something like that. Helen smiled and disengaged herself from me, then came crawling on over to my end. She placed her head on my chest and curled up like a small girl seeking safety, which she probably was. We lay there for a few minutes, nearly dozing off, but then grew chill and decided to get out of the tub.

We dressed silently in the bathroom, our water-wrinkled bodies redolent of a pool locker room. I hopped around on one foot trying to get into my pants. Helen giggled.

"Don't assault my dignity," I told her. We beamed at our reflections in the mirror, happy and more than a little confused.

Five minutes later, seated on a stool in the kitchen, I remembered what I was doing in California: investigating the murder of Helen's husband. I felt no guilt, just a little negligence. The widow was spooning coffee into a percolator, her red hair spilling over a green dressing gown.

"Helen, do you have Carpenter's address?" I asked.

"Dale?"

"Yeah, the cowboy."

"I'm sure we do. Why?"

"I want to go see him."

She finished measuring out the coffee and plugged in the pot. "Right now?"

"Right after coffee. I saw him earlier today at Parker's and I want to follow it up."

Her eyes widened. "You didn't tell me Dale was there," she said. "What was he doing?"

"A very relevant question. That's why I'd like to chat with him. I saw Carpenter ring Parker's bell. Parker came to the door and looked every bit as happy as if his fillings had just fallen out. But that's all I know because that's when my head came off."

"Should I call Dale and tell him you want to see him?"

"Thanks, no. I'd prefer to sneak up on him. I don't really have the slightest idea why he visited Parker today, but it's not necessarily kosher. You call him and he'll just have time to invent excuses."

"You think he might be in trouble?"

"Definitely."

The coffee was mediocre, as it always is out of a percolator, but Helen's intentions were the best. We sat at the kitchen table and held hands. I was very tired. It was ten-thirty and I knew that if I didn't leave immediately, I'd go find myself a blanket and fade away. So I kissed the lady's cheek and got up.

"It wasn't very good coffee, was it?" she asked. "You can be honest."

"Passable coffee, superb service. You going to be all right here alone?"

She shrugged. I don't think it had occurred to her that she would be by herself.

"I guess so. Could I come with you?"

"I'd prefer that you didn't. Let's not get into a 'Thin Man' routine, not yet. You could use some peace and quiet. I'll be back soon."

She took my arm.

"How soon?"

"Soon enough."

"I'll read in the meantime."

Helen looked up Carpenter's address—in the Hollywood Hills—and wrote out directions, then walked me to the door.

"Lock up," I told her. "Front and back."

"Stop trying to scare me, Jack," she said chidingly. "I don't need it, really."

"I'm being realistic. Something nuts is going on and I don't want you hurt. If there's a gun in the house . . ."

"There is."

"Then keep it handy and don't let anyone in but me."

I had made her afraid. It was for her own welfare, but I didn't enjoy doing it.

"Hurry back."

I gave her nose a little pinch and left. Walking down the steps, I heard the bolts locking shut behind me. It was, and wasn't, a comforting sound.

9

The slip of paper said 20 Mockingbird Lane and it was a fifteen-minute drive from Adrian's house. Or should have been, according to Helen. I found myself driving in slow, majestic circles for an additional fifteen, before finding the little cul-de-sac off Doheny.

Mockingbird was a small, thickly wooded street, with perhaps a half-dozen large homes on each side. The homes looked to be of recent origin; new money had come here, with architect's plans, yellow bulldozers, and picture windows. Mounds of earth were still piled up next to several of the homes; one was only three-quarters finished.

Number 20 was at the very end of the street, which dropped off behind concrete and chicken wire to a striking view of Beverly Hills below. I parked the Chrysler by the overlook and got out. The rain had ended and the sky was clearing; some stars had appeared. I walked over to the fence and looked down over the quiet wealthy glow of Beverly Hills. I could see where the neon fire of the Strip ended and the muted, pearly street lamps of the Hills began. Los Angeles. I still had no sense of it, no handle. For two and a half days, I had been wandering through a fun house, losing myself, forgetting my mission for hours at a time. All I knew was that Walter was dead and that he had been a Communist, and that his death was significant enough to bring the FBI and Congress into the act. Beyond those facts and the fact of two serious attempts on my life, I didn't know a goddamn thing.

I turned and headed up the two-dozen winding steps to Carpenter's house. It was a large ranch-style affair, built on two levels, rising on the right side to a connected pool house. When I got to the top of the stairs, I caught a blue glimpse of pool, brightly dappled by breeze and underwater lights. The house had a Southwestern look, constructed at sharp jutting angles of a bleached-out pine that suggested mesas, cactus, and a canopy of cloudless sky. Bull's horns adorned the front door, hinged into a doorknocker. I pulled the horns down and knocked twice.

I waited. The lights were on inside but I heard no movement to the door, heard no splashing out by the pool. I studied my shoes and knocked again. More silence. Another rap of the bull's horns and then I called Carpenter's name. My shout sounded empty. I continued to wait. Maybe he was in the sack, with a starlet or a young ranch hand. It would take time to put on his robe, get into his slippers . . .

After the fourth knock, I tried the door. It was unlocked and opened into the living room.

The place was an unholy mess.

Everything had been turned on its ear: chairs, sofa cushions, fire irons, wastebaskets, liquor bottles, wine glasses, books, papers, folders, and manila envelopes, scattered with a hurricane's logic across the length and breadth of the wood-paneled room. Only a pair of pearl-handled revolvers, long-barreled beauties circa 1860, stood undisturbed on mountings over the fireplace.

I entered the room and closed the door behind me. It was quiet enough to hear your own pulse. I stepped around a fallen rocker and surveyed the ruins. The work had been done frantically, objects flung wildly across the room, like the fireplace shovel, twenty feet from the fireplace, lying beneath a gouge it had made in the paneling. I picked the shovel up; it was not light. Somebody had been in a great hurry, or very frustrated, or both of the above.

I cleared my throat and called Carpenter's name again, expecting, and receiving, no answer. I placed my right hand on the Colt revolver snoozing peacefully beneath my left armpit and started down the hall leading to the rest of the house.

First door on the left was a bathroom. The shower was still dripping and the cover of the toilet tank was ajar. Next to the bathroom was a guest bedroom. The closet had been emptied of old suits, hangers, and bags full of mothballs. A queen-sized mattress had been lifted and thrown over the foot of the brass bed. Drawers, shirts, and underwear had been hurled across the floor. I backed out of the room and continued on down the hallway. It was like visiting a museum of chaos.

Except that the master bedroom—a large, airy domicile with French doors leading out to a patio—was as perfectly neat and tucked-in as if the maid had just made her dutiful exit. There were two explanations for this: a sudden arrival had scared off the intruders, or said intruders had found what they were looking for.

I backed out of the bedroom and into the hallway. It veered off at a right angle from that spot, rising four steps and leading out to the poolhouse through a glass door, which was open. The poolhouse had showers, marked "Fillies" and "Stallions," a long bar lined with wicker stools, and a picture window overlooking Beverly Hills. If this was communism, it looked pretty good to me.

Another sliding glass door led out to the pool. I went outside and followed a flagstone path that wound around a group of azalea bushes. It led me to the pool.

It was a handsome pool; the water looked inviting, a mild breeze breaking its blue surface into illuminated ripples. Ribbons of light shimmered across its face and fallen leaves spun slowly about in a whirlpool near the diving board. A pump, housed in a wooden shed, droned mechanically. The sky continued to clear, stars growing sharper and brighter and it would have been a swell night for a party. But the host wasn't feeling very well. Dale Carpenter, sitting in a canvas chair at poolside, was as dead as Louis XIV.

Not *as* dead, exactly. Louie had a big headstart on Carpenter who, by the looks of it, had only checked out a few hours before. But that's mere quibbling; the cowboy was plenty dead, shot through the chest, with no director around to say "cut!" and no wardrobe gal to dust off his pants when he got up off the ground. This was for ugly real, sitting in a chair next to his own pool, dressed in plaid swim trunks and a yellow terrycloth jacket—yellow with blotches of red. His knees were scraped; it seemed a fair assumption that he had been returned to the chair after falling over. Another fair assumption was that he had been killed by a thorough professional: two shots had done the job and one would have been sufficient. They were bull's-eyes through the heart. Carpenter's eyes were open and he was leaning against the side of the chair, as if listening to an amusing story.

I took it all in and tossed it around. A few quick thoughts surfaced: whoever had skulled me had seen Carpenter go into Parker's house with the manila envelope. The actor had most certainly discovered something of importance and had brought it—for reasons I dearly wanted to know—to Parker's attention. He had spoken with Parker and then returned home, watched all the while. Tired and strained from the day's events, Carpenter changed into his trunks and went outside for a refreshing swim. When he climbed out of the pool, a marksman appeared and killed him. The house was searched; after ransacking the living room and guest room, the searcher or searchers found what he or they had come for and departed.

But the unknowns were staggering: what was in the envelop the cowboy star had been carrying? Why had he gone to see Parker? Was the Parker house under surveillance? Was Carpenter being followed? Was I? I'd swear to the fact that no one had tailed me; it's the kind of thing I usually notice. But it didn't really make much difference; Carpenter was dead and Parker remained the key to the whole shebang. And I began to have doubts about Parker's life expectancy as well; he had looked not merely appalled when the actor rang his bell, he looked frightened. I didn't feel so hot myself. It was nearing midnight, time to get back to Helen, time to leave Carpenter and call the cops. Anonymously, of course. Finding one stiff had caused me enough grief; catching the daily double raised the grim prospect of my becoming Homicide's plumpest turkey.

I left the way I came, whipping out a hanky and smearing the doorknobs I had touched. Sure, it might have destroyed evidence, but I was goddamned if I was going to leave my prints all over the place. Besides which, the professional manner of the actor's death led me to believe that he was dispatched by people who did such things wearing gloves. Like Mickey Mouse.

After closing the front door, I descended the stairs, through a green passageway of sculpted shrubs. The bushes were trimmed in exotic parabolas, not a twig was out of place. Only a single stray piece of paper broke the symmetry, a scrap that had nestled in the lower branches near the bottom of the stairs. Being a curious fellow, I reached down and picked up the scrap.

It was a newspaper clipping, an old one. It was brittle and yellow and incomplete, its ragged edges indicating disintegration, rather than tearing or scissoring. I went to the Chrysler and read it while lying down in the front seat.

"Pardee's arrest on the rape charge," it began, "is his second listed offense, according to Denver authorities. He was charged with disturbing the peace during a New Year's fracas at the Big Sky Club in 1927, an incident which . . ." And that was it.

I turned it over, saw "POST" but no date. Maybe it was nothing at all, just something blown from a passing garbage truck, but my light turned red. Stop. Think this over. Forget the garbage truck. Let's say this had fallen from a folder held by a man running down these very stairs, say, a couple of hours ago. Let us say, further, that the man had just committed a capital crime and was too preoccupied to notice the little scrap drop from the folder or envelope.

I placed the clipping in my wallet, certain that it was worth a large stack of chips.

I phoned the L.A. cops from a pay booth on Sunset, then drove back to Sherman Oaks, winding around the long dangerous curves of Mulholland Drive. It took longer than I had anticipated and I suddenly got anxious, terribly so, about Helen sitting all alone in that big house on Escadero. I wanted to speed things up, but that was asking for a trip back East in the baggage car, so I took the curves as well as I could, furious at myself for leaving Helen so vulnerable. My state of mind grew increasingly agitated, bordering on the frantic, and I began tearing about like a drunken stunt driver, stomping on the brakes, squealing around bends—virtually two-wheeling an awful curve near Franklin Canyon—in a solo race against my fevered imagination.

And I was dog-tired to boot, at the smoldering end of a long, mean, and frustrating day, in which my own death had nearly been sandwiched between Adrian's funeral and Carpenter's murder. I had been beaten on the head, I had made love to Walter's wife, and now, finally, I had lost my balance.

I pulled into Escadero Drive doing around sixty, and left a foothill of rubber in the Adrian driveway as I floored the brake pedal. The Chrysler shrieked to a stop and I had to hold out a hand to avoid getting creased by the dashboard. I jumped from the car and ran toward the house. Only a dim light shone through a downstairs window, but the top story was bright and full of welcome. I went up the front stairs positively ballooning with dread, legs shaking as I rang the bell. I rang it twice in quick succession.

"Jack?" I heard Helen call from inside.

"Yeah!" My voice was as unsteady as my knees, which rattled from relief and weariness. I had given out.

She opened the door, alive and well.

"How was it?" she asked. I went inside and headed up the stairs, pretending not to hear. It was more than I could handle right now.

I started down the hall to the study, but Helen had moved my things into the master bedroom. When I entered her room, she handed me a towel.

"Check-out time at noon," she told me.

I washed up quickly, whipped off my clothes, and tumbled into the sack, snuggling beneath the blanket like a child. Helen got in and wrapped herself tightly about me. We lay there like a pair of overgrown embryos.

"Missed you," she whispered.

I grunted in reply and dug deeper beneath the blanket. My eyelids closed like stone weights and I was asleep before Helen had a chance to turn off the table lamp. Asleep before she had another chance to ask me about Dale Carpenter.

I broke the news to Helen the next morning, before she saw the paper. It seemed to me that she took it well.

"Oh Christ," she said, then sighed. She stuck a thumbnail into her lovely mouth and chewed on it.

We were sitting in something called a breakfast nook, a sun-washed corner of the Adrian kitchen into which a red banquette had been built. Potted geraniums stood on the window ledges and a group of jays were having a small party in the garden outside. The sky was blue and generous and the sun warmed my back right through the window. It was a thoroughly magnificent morning. Helen in her flowered robe and I in my tan slacks and blue sports shirt, bent over porcelain cups, could have been posing for a feature spread in *Better Homes and Gardens.* Politely chewing our French toast-SNAP, discussing plans for the day-SNAP, turning to observe the musical cavorting of the jays-SNAP. A handsome couple, beneficiaries of America's largesse, having found their literal place in the sun: a radiant California breakfast nook.

"You found him dead?" Helen asked.

"Uh-huh. But that's between you, me, and the geraniums."

"Did you call the police?"

"From a pay phone on Sunset, anonymously."

Helen lowered her head and stared into her coffee. The sunlight made her fair skin almost opaque and turned her red hair into a virtual crown. A teardrop formed at the tip of her nose, hung tenuously for a second, then dropped soundlessly into her cup. She spread her hands over her face and wept. "Jack, this is so awful."

It was that. I put my hand into the crook of her arm and squeezed as gently as I knew how. "It plain stinks, Helen. It's rotten. Were you and Walter close to the guy?"

Helen kept her face covered but shook her head in the negative. I clammed up and let her cry it out. She stopped after another minute or two, removing her hands unapologetically and facing me with damp cheeks and glistening eyes. She blew her nose into a paper napkin, so noisily that it made the both of us smile.

"God, Jack," she said, taking my hand. "What a time you're having out here. It was nice of us to invite you."

"It's been some fish fry. I was getting bored in New York, but this has been a bit more than I anticipated."

"Maybe things will calm down now."

"Maybe. I wouldn't bet on it." I poured myself some more coffee. "Tell me about your relationship to Carpenter."

"We weren't very close to him. We'd see him with the others in the group, of course, but never individually. He wasn't terribly bright; very earnest, but obvious, you know? Always discovering things that everybody else had known for years and making a big to-do over them. Like

128

the power company was gypping people or some local politician was a crook. Stuff like that."

"I know the type."

"But he was a sweet guy, basically, very sincere. I'm not sure about his sex life. No one was, I think. But that's par for the course out here, you don't even give it a second thought." She mulled that over. "No chance it was one of those kind of murders, is there, Jack?"

"You mean where a guy brings home a sailor who turns out to be a psycho? I don't think so. The trip Carpenter made to Parker's house, the way the house had been gone through, this thing . . ." I took out my wallet and removed the clipping about the Denver man named Pardee. "I found this in the hedges outside Carpenter's place and I'm surmising, just for the hell of it, that it flew out of a manila envelope or folder being carried down the steps by the killer."

Helen took the clipping and examined it carefully, turning it over, reading it twice, moving her lips. After studying it a third time, she looked up, her face registering no sale.

"What do you think it is?" she asked.

"God knows. I'm assuming it's a lead until I find out different."

"That's how detectives work?"

"That's how I work." I was showing off and Helen knew it. She smiled.

"My little Sherlock Holmes."

She took my hand and kissed it. That hadn't happened in a long, long while. I liked it very much.

We sat holding hands in the breakfast nook and all I really wanted to do was toss Helen Adrian over my shoulder and take her home to Sunnyside. Then the telephone started ringing and my day began sliding downhill.

Helen got up and answered the phone.

"Yes, he is." She pointed at me. "I'll see if I can get him." She put the phone down on the counter and whispered, "Police."

129

"Ah, shit." I couldn't get a break.

"You want me to tell them you left for the day?"

I thought about it. "The hell with it," I finally said, getting up. "I'll have to talk to them sooner or later."

"About Dale?"

"Sure. I just hope they keep it short."

My pal Wynn was at the other end.

"Hate to bother you on such a beautiful morning, LeVine."

"That's okay. I was starting to think you didn't like me anymore."

"Seen the papers yet?"

"Nope. I was just having breakfast with Mrs. Adrian. How'd you know I was here?"

"We're the police. We know things."

"I'm not sure I follow your logic."

"I'll laugh some other time. Listen, LeVine, Dale Carpenter, the actor, has been murdered."

I silently counted to five.

"Christ almighty. When?"

"Sometime yesterday evening. That's what the coroner says. We got a tip last night around midnight and found him dead next to his swimming pool."

"No suicide this time?"

"Not so funny. We'd like to talk with you this morning."

"Who's 'we'?"

"People. You're the one who was selling murder in the Adrian case. This appears to be a related matter, although that's strictly between us. Strictly. Actually I'm surprised one of Mrs. Adrian's friends didn't call her when they saw the paper. Very surprised."

"Could be her friends don't want to bother her. Day after the funeral and all."

"What happened, Mr. LeVine?" Helen called out to me, her long fingers cradling her coffee cup. She was really something.

"In a minute, Mrs. Adrian," I called back. "Listen,

Wynn, let me off. This isn't going to be any fun. When do you want me?"

"It's 9:15 now. Be here by ten."

"Thanks. I thought you were going to rush me."

"Stop being a pain in the ass. Quarter past ten the latest."

He hung up. Helen beamed at me.

"Was that a good thing to do?" she asked.

"You're full of surprises." I sat down beside her. "That was our friend Lieutenant Wynn. He couldn't believe we hadn't heard about Carpenter. Maybe he still can't, but thanks for trying."

"You think you might take me in as a partner, Jack?" Helen smiled as she said it, but the question was a mile-long freight train, hauling doubts, hesitations, and hopes across a strange new landscape. I remembered again that this was a woman whose husband had died two and a half days ago.

I stroked her cheek.

"You want to be a detective?"

She shrugged. "I think I'd like to spend some time with you, but I'm confused."

"Me too. So let's just let things ride, okay?"

"Okay." She caught my hand and squeezed it.

The doorbell rang and Helen got up. "That'll be the Wohls," she said. "They're going to spend the day with me. You want to see them?"

"Not right now."

"Then go out through the back. If they ask, I'll say the police wanted you."

She gave me a wifely peck on the brow and went to the front. I headed out the kitchen door into the garden. It looked and smelled as rich and clean as the day the first primordial creatures slid, swam, and waddled their way to the muddy banks of the earth and began screwing things up. I waited a couple of beats, then walked around the path to the front, where I got into the Chrysler and started off. I was curious to find out exactly what the cops were figuring. In exchange, I was prepared to tell them not a solitary thing.

10

They wanted me there at 10:15 sharp in order to keep me waiting on a green bench for an hour. I loathe cops. It's a blanket indictment, I know, and people tell me that there are plenty of decent guys walking neighborhood beats, helping old women up that last step, letting small children play with their nightsticks, and I've even met one or two. Joe Egan, of my local Sunnyside precinct, is a fine and witty gentleman; given a few minutes, I might come up with a dozen more names. But for sheer calculated rudeness, for pomposity and self-importance, for imbecility, for toadying to superiors and kicking the pants of inferiors, you have to go a long way to beat the officers of the law. In twenty years of private sleuthing, I've had so goddamn many unpleasant, underhanded, and depressing encounters with homicide dicks and robbery squads that I'm beyond the point of retrieval. And I still can't get used to the lack of ordinary civility.

I asked the guy at the desk when he thought they'd be ready for me. He laughed.

"They'll let me know and I'll let you know, okay?" He

had thinning black hair and bleary, humorless eyes. A crossword puzzle was spread out before him.

I passed most of the hour reading the paper. A front-page headline announced the grisly curtain-ringer to Dale Carpenter's life and career, complete with two pictures of the star: a head shot and a publicity still of Carpenter feeding a palomino. "His well-muscled body, clothed in a yellow lounging robe and plaid swim trunks, was found next to the swimming pool of his luxurious ranch-style home in the Hollywood Hills." Reporter Pat Marks went on to describe the "shambles" inside the home and to spill the official police verdict: Carpenter had been killed by burglars. The place had been gone through with such violent abandon that robbery was a credible motive. I happened not to believe it and wondered if the police did.

By 11:30 I was reduced to reading the horoscopes. Mine recommended "decisive action." So I got up and headed for the door. "Tell Wynn he knows where to reach me," I told the desk man. "I've got things to do."

He looked up from his puzzle. "Hold it. You can't just come in and out. They want to see you."

"Then you call Wynn right now and tell him I either go up now or go home now."

He scratched his head. "I'll do you a favor and call," he said unhappily, "but they don't like me to do it."

The desk man picked up the phone just as a pair of swinging double doors at the end of the room opened up. Wynn entered, followed by his faithful Lemon and Caputo. The three of them were wearing brown suits. Wynn clapped me on the back, friendly-like.

"Sorry, LeVine, but it's been a madhouse this morning. We couldn't bring you up any sooner."

"Of course not. That's why I had to be here at a quarter past ten. Must be hell, though, with this Carpenter robbery breaking. You find out what was stolen?"

Wynn's eyes narrowed. He removed a pipe from his breast pocket and banged it out on his heel.

"You have some ideas about this, LeVine?" he asked.

"I have ideas about everything, but I don't talk about them in waiting rooms."

The lieutenant turned and shouted "Let's go" to Lemon and Caputo, who were having a big laugh with the desk man. Something about why a fireman wears red suspenders. They came trotting over to Wynn's side, inevitably flanking him. They were like a dog act, those boys.

"We're going somewhere," Wynn told me.

"I already had breakfast."

He begrudged himself a small smile.

"Some people would like to talk with you. C'mon."

The lieutenant turned on his heel and started for a rear exit. Lemon and Caputo held back, so I fell into step, a prisoner's cadence, and the four of us went through a back door and out into the headquarters' large parking lot. The lot was completely enclosed but for a manned gate, bordered on four sides by a rust-orange concrete wall. It looked like the exercise yard of the Big House.

We got into an unmarked black sedan, a Ford. Wynn and I climbed into the back, while the meatheads argued over whose turn it was to drive.

"C'mon, you dumb bastards, let's get going," barked Wynn.

Lemon finally slid in on the driver's side. Caputo sulked.

"I drive the next time," he insisted.

The ride proceeded in relative quiet. I attempted to make conversation, but Wynn only grunted and sucked on his pipe. He clearly did not want to talk about the Carpenter murder.

"If you're so sure it was robbery," I droned on, delighted to make a pest of myself, "why call me in? You think I'm a fence or something? I don't even live in this miserable city."

Wynn blew pipe smoke in my face, on purpose.

"And another thing," I brayed on, "why can't you tell

me who I'm meeting with. I'm about to see them anyway. What's all the hush-hush?"

"LeVine, I wish you'd shut up. I'm trying to think," the lieutenant said softly.

"What's to think about? You got one suicide and one robbery, right? That's the whole ball game."

Wynn was being unusually restrained. He looked sour and pensive, like the manager of a sixth-place club in the late innings of the season's last game. A sense of resignation tightened the corners of his mouth into small curt creases.

"They're really screwing it up for you, aren't they, Wynn?"

He stared out the window. "In spades," he said.

I was not taken by surprise when the police car pulled up in front of the Pill Building on Omar Avenue.

"This is it, Chief," said Lemon.

Wynn leaned forward and peered out the windshield. "You sure?"

"Pill Building. Number 11 Omar."

"Jesus Christ," the lieutenant muttered. "Okay, LeVine. Out."

"Some nice place," I said. "What have they got, Hitler locked up in the basement?"

"Don't give me a hard time, peeper, please. I'm plenty ticked off as it is."

I did Wynn the favor of getting off his back. The four of us stepped from the unmarked sedan, Wynn blinking in the bright sunlight and buttoning his suit jacket. I followed him into the filthy lobby of the Pill Building, Lemon and Caputo covering our rear flank.

"Holy Christmas," said Wynn disgustedly. "What a fucking dump."

"We don't do things like this in New York," I said cheerfully. "Skulk around in unmarked cars, meet secretly in dustbins."

Wynn didn't answer me, but stood staring down at the

floor. A large waterbug cakewalked around his shoe, but the cop didn't notice. He just waited, with increased agitation, for the elevator to arrive. The needle, as if magnetized, was stuck on three. Wynn leaned on the bell; it rang like a fire alarm in the empty shaft.

"Goddamn it!" Wynn screamed.

I turned to Lemon.

"Why don't you suggest that we utilize the stairway?"

Wynn glared at me and started up the stairs. He was terribly angry. For all my obnoxious chatter, I felt a little sorry for the guy. Just a little.

It was the same office: Haller's antique and jewelry appraisal service. Wynn knocked once, waited, then knocked twice.

"We auditioning for a spy movie?" I asked.

The door opened and the man I had observed yesterday, the one with the sunglasses and buttonhole mouth, stood to one side, hand on the knob.

"Lieutenant," he said pleasantly. "Gentlemen."

"Davis," said Wynn, shaking his hand and entering the room. The rest of us followed. Seated in a corner of the office, in an ancient, cracked leather chair, was the younger man, he of the baby-fat jowls and ill-fitting suits. He arose and was introduced as U.S. Congressman Richard M. Nixon. Nixon shook hands all around, starting with Wynn and ending with me. I kept my mouth shut.

"And I'm P. J. Davis," the other man announced. "I'm an investigator employed by the House Committee on Un-American Activities. Why don't we all make ourselves comfortable."

The six of us sat down, pulling up various "easy" chairs and folding ass-breakers. I couldn't have gotten comfortable if I had planted myself atop a stack of satin pillows. The atmosphere was distinctly unpleasant. Not hostile, or even slightly angry; there was just that unmistakable air of crossed purposes. Everyone was on edge and expecting to be lied to, everyone was unsure as to what the other knew. It was like sitting down to play poker and discovering that the deck contained sixty cards.

I lit up a Lucky and looked out the window. Across the street, a small boy was riding his tricycle around a backyard littered with the artifacts of poverty: the rusting, blind carcass of a Plymouth, a broken washing machine, a small mound of soda bottles and clothespins. The kid looked very happy.

Davis cleared his throat and began speaking in a schoolteacher's humoring tone of voice. "Mr. Levine would probably like to know why the congressman and I wished to see him this morning," he began.

"It's LeVine," I told him. "Like Hollywood and Vine."

"That's an unusual name," he replied with a salesman's smile.

"So's P. J. I don't think I ever met one before."

"Patrick Jefferson."

"Very patriotic."

He chuckled moderately and I flashed an extremely charming and engaging grin. Congressman Nixon smiled. Wynn nervously tapped his fingers together. Lemon and Caputo watched their knees.

"Lieutenant," Davis said to Wynn, "are we all going to discuss this matter?"

"No." He snapped his fingers at Lemon and Caputo. "Fellas, go wait in the hall."

The two cops nodded heavily, like horses, then arose and left the room, leaving the four of us to sit in silence.

"Okay, LeVine," Wynn finally said. "We're going along with you. Adrian was murdered."

The three men looked at me for guidance and wisdom.

"What am I supposed to say, thank you?"

"Of course not," Davis answered smoothly.

Nixon spoke up for the first time.

"You're from New York City, Mr. LeVine?"

"That's right, congressman."

"I have a great many friends there," he informed me.

I nodded and kept my silence. Wynn coughed. We sat quietly on our chairs, as polite and apprehensive as young girls waiting to be asked to dance.

"Why do you think Adrian was murdered?" Davis finally asked.

"I don't think I ever said that definitively. What I said was that murder was not to be ruled out."

"And you think it was ruled out?" he went on.

"Everything Lieutenant Wynn told me indicated that it was, yes."

"But perhaps the lieutenant was giving such indications for a reason?"

"Perhaps. Why don't you ask him?"

Davis didn't want to ask him and Wynn didn't want to be asked. The reason was plain enough: Wynn hadn't pursued the homicide angle because he had been told not to. Davis knew it and was being a chump to grill me about it.

"All right then," the investigator continued. "Let's say that you *suspected* Adrian might have been murdered."

I was getting bored.

"Listen," I began, "if this is leading somewhere, why don't we skip the prelims and get to the main event. That's what the fans paid to see."

"Keep your shirt on, LeVine," said Wynn, stuffing a pipe into his face.

I shrugged in the direction of Nixon. He batted his eyelashes, then leaned over and reached into a black briefcase, his long fingers extending from an oversized sports jacket that covered his arm almost to the first knuckle. He removed a yellow legal pad from the briefcase, then balanced it against a crossed knee.

"I like to keep a record," he said to no one in particular.

I couldn't quite get a handle on the congressman. He seemed painfully shy and looked, from a certain angle, like a college debater. But he also had the shifting gaze and blue jowls of a baby-faced con.

"Let me assure you," Davis said curtly, "that we're heading for what you call the 'main event.' And let me remind you that you are addressing individuals entrusted with a top-level congressional investigation."

"Into communism in the movie colony?" I asked.

Davis nodded solemnly. "That is correct. So let me ask again why you suspected that Walter Adrian might have been murdered."

"Because suicide didn't wash."

"Why not?"

"It just didn't seem like him. I didn't think it was impossible, just unlikely."

"Did you think, perhaps, that he had been killed by a Communist agent?"

I know that I shouldn't have, but I smiled. A big, wide, fat-pussycat smile. After overhearing that bizarre conversation yesterday, I knew the way these birds were thinking, but it still sounded like a hashish dream to me.

"You've seen too many movies," I said.

Davis pulled his chair closer to mine and began raising his voice.

"Mr. LeVine, we are acquainted with your background and your sympathies. Thus, we are not surprised by your cavalier, mocking dismissal of the Red menace. However, let me warn you . . ."

I decided to cut him off. "Hold it right there, okay? Fine. Now you want me to answer questions about the deaths of Adrian or Carpenter and I'll answer them to the best of my knowledge and ability. In fact, to cut right to the quick, I'll tell you right off the bat that I don't see any double knock-off engineered by the Communists, the Red menace, or Red Ruffing. That's one thing. As to my 'background,'

Wynn already tried that number, complete with FBI files and it was a horse laugh then. I again cheerfully confess, *mea culpa,* to having signed a petition protesting the frying of those two poor organ-grinders in Boston and, yes, it was me who sent that rice and bean money to the Spanish refugees. As an added bonus, I'll also reveal that I voted for Roosevelt the first two times and nobody the last two times, and that I miss Fiorello LaGuardia."

Nixon was taking it all down.

"That's two 'l's' in Fiorello," I told him, rising from my chair, "and a capital 'g.' "

"Yes, I know," he answered politely.

"Why are you standing, LeVine?" asked Wynn.

"Because I'm leaving, unless we get to the point."

Davis waved his hand.

"Sit down, LeVine," he said. "You're in no position to walk out on us. I don't want to pull rank, but this, *ex officio,* is part of a congressional investigation. If you don't want to talk to us now, we'll call you into sworn session. You might prefer that, I don't know. I thought this would be easier."

I sat down. Davis turned to Nixon.

"Congressman, I wonder if we should show Mr. LeVine the Bureau memo on the Carpenter matter?"

Nixon pursed his lips in thought. "I think that would be advisable," he said with a judicious nod of the head. The congressman reached those long fingers into his briefcase—I swear he could have used his sleeves for mittens, they were that long—and extracted a pink sheet of paper. He studied it, nodding all the while, then rose from his chair and handed the sheet to Davis, whispering into the investigator's ear.

"Of course," Davis said out loud, as if on the telephone. "Absolutely."

Nixon stopped whispering. Davis studied the sheet. Wynn got up and looked over his shoulder, without much interest. I beamed at Nixon, who returned a tight-lipped smile.

"Lovely weather out here," I told him. "It's my first trip to these parts."

"Oh, is it?" he answered brightly. "Well, this is the best weather in the world. I was in the Navy, you know, and we went all over the world, but this is the best weather. Quite frankly, I almost regret getting elected to Congress and having to be away from the sunshine so much."

"Tough break," I concurred.

Davis leaned forward and handed me the sheet. It was a memo, on FBI letterhead.

> TO: P. J. DAVIS
>
> FROM: CLARENCE WHITE
>
> RE: CARPENTER HOMICIDE
>
> Highly placed operatives in the Hollywood CP have indicated to us that Dale Carpenter, like Walter Adrian, was murdered on orders direct from the highest levels in Moscow . . .

"Wait a minute," I said to Wynn. "Did you know all the while that Adrian had been murdered by Moscow?"

Wynn shrugged and Davis looked embarrassed.

"No, he did not," the investigator said, "and I will tell you why. This is highly, *highly* secret information. When the FBI first learned of the true facts behind Adrian's death, it was necessary to keep that information at the very top levels of the Bureau and the House Committee on Un-American Activities. The police were not informed."

"They were just told to lay off the case and call it a suicide?"

Davis ignored my question.

"But the murder of Carpenter," he continued, in a voice of doom, "which was more obviously an instance of homicide, made it imperative that tight cooperation and absolute trust between the Committee, the Bureau, and the L.A. police would be necessary to keep the lid on."

"Which is why Carpenter's death is attributed to robbery?" I asked.

"Of course," said Davis.

"You going to dig up a suspect?" I asked Wynn.

"Maybe, maybe not," he answered dryly.

"Lot of publicity. You're going to have to stick it to someone. Don't you have a boxcar full of Mexicans for occasions like this?"

Wynn did not appreciate my needling and told me to shut up.

"Please, gentlemen," Nixon interjected. "I think Mr. LeVine should finish reading the memo."

I returned to the pink sheet.

> It was reported that Carpenter, like Adrian, was about to renounce his Party membership and expose the inner workings of the Communist apparatus in the motion picture industry. There is no certainty as to whether the two homicides were committed by a United States or a Soviet national, but the former seems a more likely probability, as it is doubtful that the Russians would risk discovery.

> The key Hollywood CP members—such as Wohl, Arthur, and Perillo—are reportedly in panic and are being kept under surveillance. It is unlikely that local Party members will cooperate with your Committee's efforts. The familiar Soviet pattern of methodical terror as a means of enforcing discipline is evident.

The memo was initialed "C.W."

"Who's White?" I asked. "He's the same guy who put together that memo on me."

"Clarence White," Davis said solemnly, "has never been seen by any of us. Dramatic as that may sound, it is true. He is chief of the undercover unit that has been investigating subversion in Hollywood since the middle of the war." He watched my eyebrows rise and smiled. "Oh yes, Mr. LeVine, for that long. You see, the unit was studying the possibilities of German subversion out here. Early on, it perceived that the real threat was coming from the left, not the right, and it began concentrating on that side of the fence. There are memos White wrote in 1944 that are absolutely prophetic. Of course, no one was listening to him then. He was considered something of an eccentric, in fact, and was almost switched to another assignment."

"Had White been listened to, a great deal of hardship, a *very* great deal," said Nixon, emphasizing his words with an umpire's sweep of the hands, "could have been avoided."

"So White has infiltrated the Party in some manner?" I asked.

"He's chief of the Bureau unit studying subversion in Hollywood," Davis said, "and that's all you need to know."

He got up and began pacing, a little theatrically, I thought.

"What exactly is your function in this matter, Mr. Le-Vine?" he finally asked.

"I'm conducting an investigation of Adrian's death on behalf of his widow."

"Do you plan to help us?"

"Insofar as you are investigating Walter's death, per-haps. But I'm not on a Red hunt."

"This has become a matter affecting the domestic security of the United States, Mr. LeVine." This was Nixon and there was now a distinctly unfriendly edge to his voice.

"That's your job," I told him, "not mine. I'm a private dick checking out a friend's murder. Period."

Nixon leaned over and began rummaging through his briefcase. Davis sat down and cracked his knuckles. Wynn went over to the window. Looked like the party was breaking up.

"All right, LeVine," Davis said. "You can go."

"Anybody going to follow me?"

"No," the investigator said firmly, "but you may come to regret treating this matter so lightly."

"How so?"

"Because you just might." And that was all the answer I was going to get. Davis gestured toward the door. "Good afternoon, LeVine."

I stood up. "I'm waiting for Wynn. He's my ride."

"He'll be with you in a moment," Davis said evenly. "Just step out in the hall. Lieutenant Wynn will join you after he speaks with us."

"Wonderful," I told him, then walked over to where Nixon was seated. "So long, congressman."

Nixon got up and extended his hand; it was quite wet. "Thank you for your help, Mr. LeVine," he began earnestly. "I would like to make one observation, however. A great many people from the East—sincere, well-meaning people, I'm sure," and here he shook his face for emphasis, "seem to think that the House Committee is going to conduct some kind of 'witchhunt.' Nothing could be further from the truth.

"People from the East—and I'm not condemning them, you understand—many of them say 'Oh, these are just a bunch of politicians looking for the headlines, looking for votes.' " He wouldn't let go of my hand. "Mr. LeVine, I wish that were true. I wish it was just something for headlines, for the papers.

"But you see," and now he looked me straight in the eye, "it isn't like that at all. Mr. LeVine, America is facing the greatest national security crisis in her history. That's why people in positions of responsibility and public trust, people like myself, for instance," he blinked a few times, "are taking this matter so very seriously. I'm not criticizing you in any way, Mr. LeVine. You have your right to disagree and that's what makes America great. What I am saying is that your right to disagree will be endangered if the Soviet program for world domination progresses any further."

Nixon let go of my hand.

"Thanks for the tip," I told him, and left the room.

It was a relief to stand outside with Lemon and Caputo, leaning against the wall like kids outside the principal's office. The two cops were stupid, but at least they weren't crazy.

11

It was around 1:30 when I returned to the Chrysler. It was parked in front of the police station. Wynn had remained in a foul temper all the way back and was glad to be rid of me. He and the department were being manipulated and he knew that I knew it. I was a walking and kibbitzing reminder of his impotence.

So Wynn just dropped me off with a final "Stay out of my hair!" and I climbed into the Chrysler. All dressed up and no place to go. The morning's activities had been a diverting political science lesson, but I had learned nothing of use, nothing I could take in my hands like a divining rod and follow around. I was traveling on vapor, on hunches and guesswork tied together by baseless assumptions. The lack of solid leads this far into the case set my teeth on edge.

I sat unhappily in the car, attempting to devise an agenda for the remainder of the afternoon. Two obvious, though probably futile, tasks came immediately to mind: first, to get in touch with Johnny Parker and find out why the late Dale Carpenter had leaned on his bell yesterday afternoon, and second, take a shot at getting the full story behind the *Denver Post* clipping. I didn't really expect results on either.

Hunger asserted itself at that point and the tourist in me decided to have lunch at Schwab's Pharmacy, the landmark on Sunset where star-struck off-duty carhops and ushers sit nursing phosphates, waiting for Fate's sudden tap on the shoulder. The rarity of such taps hasn't hurt Schwab's business any; the joint remains one of America's most crowded waiting rooms.

Surprisingly enough, the food is pretty good. I wolfed down a steak sandwich that had nothing to be ashamed of, and spent another half hour over coffee and apple pie, dawdling until I felt I could reach Parker in his office. It was ten past two and he would still be hovering over his peach melba with Barbara Stanwyck or Pat O'Brien.

A fortyish waitress with chemically-induced blond hair and a kind, disappointed face filled my coffee cup for the third time, then started speaking to a small, round man beside me.

"I'm up for a bit at Metro," she told him. "A Bob Taylor picture."

"Gee, 'at's great," the fat man said. " 'At's terrific."

It was too depressing, even for me, so I got up and thumbed through the fan magazines for a few minutes.

At twenty after, I paid my tab and asked the cashier for a couple of bucks in change. The cashier was not pleased with my request, but complied. The third phone booth from the left was empty and I took it, shutting the door and activating a rattling fan.

I was stacking up my change when a well-groomed man of thirty rapped on the glass. I pushed the door open.

"What's your problem?"

"I'm expecting a call from Universal," he said in a querulous, combative voice.

"There any other booths free?"

He looked down the row of wooden cubicles, then smiled and leaned forward.

"Yes, there's one near the end you can take."

"Fine," I told him. "Call up Universal and tell them you moved." I shut the door in his face and dialed Warner Brothers.

I had been wrong about Parker. He wasn't at lunch with the stars. He wasn't even in California.

"Mr. Parker is in New York for a round of story conferences," his secretary told me.

"When is he expected back?"

"He'll return on Monday."

"Where could I reach him in New York?"

She asked again who I was.

"LeVine, the detective investigating the Adrian suicide."

Her voice turned conciliatory.

"Oh, I'm so sorry."

"I'm not a relative, just an investigator. Could you tell me where Mr. Parker is staying in New York?"

"I'm afraid I couldn't," she said pleasantly. "He does not wish that information to be divulged."

"Just this time or most times?"

A telephone began ringing at her end.

"Excuse me, Mr. LeVine, I have another call. Mr. Parker will be back in the office on Monday."

"Listen, this is a police matter and I urge you to tell me where . . ."

But she pushed a button and left me addressing my remarks to an unsympathetic dial tone. I pressed down and released the receiver, then fed the black box another nickel.

I got the operator and asked her to connect me with Denver Information. It took a while but Denver Information, sounding like Whistler's Mother, finally answered. The connection was miserable; I had the sensation of calling a small shack in the Rockies.

The old lady asked what city I wanted.

"Denver, ma. Could you give me the number of the *Denver Post*?"

"Surely could. I take the *Post* myself, don'tcha know."

She gave me the number right off the top of that sweet gray head. I thanked the lady and got the L.A. operator back. The business of reading and repeating the Denver number, then my number, the obtaining of a line to Denver, the wait until Denver picked up, the wait until the *Post* picked up, and finally, the dropping of a thunderous, chiming fistful of change into the correct slots—all of this, in our age of wonders, consumed fifteen minutes.

Fortunately, matters accelerated from that point on. I was briskly connected to the city room and an amiable fellow who, unlike any newspaperman I have ever encountered in my life, wished me a good afternoon.

"Afternoon," I replied. "My name is Jack LeVine and I'm a private detective currently operating out of Los Angeles. That's where I'm calling from."

"Yessir. Better keep it short, then. Those L.A. calls eat up the silver, don't they?"

"Certainly do. There a police reporter handy?"

"You're talking to him, Jack. Bud Murray. What can I do for you?"

"Bud, I'm interested in an event that occured in Denver during the late twenties or early thirties, a rape charge pressed against a man named Pardee."

"Did it stick?"

"I don't know a thing about it. Pardee was also charged with disturbing the peace on New Year's Eve in 1927, at a joint called the Big Sky Club."

"Hell, I disturb the peace every New Year's! What kind of a chickenshit rap is that?"

"He must have gotten way out of line. I'm basically interested in the rape charge, though, Bud."

"Doesn't ring any bells offhand, Jack. Before my time.

149

Only been in Denver since the war ended. There's some old cases that are famous, of course, but this isn't one of them."

"Anyway to check on it?"

"If you don't mind holding on, I could go downstairs to the morgue and see if we got any clippings on it."

"I'd appreciate it."

"Okay. Keep your quarters handy. I'll try and make it fast."

I held on for about five minutes, during which I was shaken down for another buck-sixty.

When Murray came back on the line, there was a note of curiosity in his voice.

"Funny thing, Jack, that file is empty. Folder's there, but nothing's inside. I asked around a little, though, and an old-timer on the copy desk said he vaguely remembered the case as dating from early '31 sometime. He wasn't positive but I'd take a flyer on it; he's usually right."

"I'm very grateful to you, Bud."

"Enough to tell me what it's all about?"

"No, but you've been a big help."

"That's what they all say," the reporter said good-naturedly. "Anyhow, if this leads you to Denver, stop on by. I always enjoy chewing the cud with big-city peepers."

"You just might see me. Thanks again."

I hung up and flew out of Schwab's. That empty folder might have been an accident, but I convinced myself with no trouble at all that its contents had been lifted. Which meant that the clipping had meaning and that, in turn, meant finding a library extensive enough to carry back issues of the Denver *Post*. I therefore climbed into the Chrysler and pointed it in the direction of that palmy oasis of higher education, the University of California at Los Angeles.

UCLA was a green and sprawling campus musical of a school located in the Westwood Village section of Los

Angeles, due west of Beverly Hills. The student body consisted of young men and women so beautiful they looked to have been summoned from Central Casting. Heartbreaking blondes with flawless skin and tanned, muscular legs walked with verve and bounce across the wide lawns, waving at tall blond men, all smiles, perfect and uncomplicated. These golden, agreeable youths seemed to me not merely a new generation, but a new variety in the evolutionary garden, a new species entirely.

To a City College dropout like myself, whose classmates had resembled white-skinned, bespectacled frogs, whose experience of co-eds was of an army of dark and large-boned girls already assuming the woeful countenances of their mothers, the spectacle of UCLA was disheartening. I felt old, ugly, and invisible. As I made my way to the library, students seemed to part around me as if stepping past a tree. Why look at a pale yid in a green hat with an army of beach boys to choose from?

I was not surprised to find the library virtually empty. Perhaps a half-dozen people were seated in the main downstairs reading room, bent over textbooks and taking notes. From their pallor, I judged them to be Easterners hiding from the radiant good looks and sunny, sexy friendship of the California kids. I probably would have done the same.

There was nobody at the main desk. I drummed my fingers and coughed: a middle-aged woman poked her head from an open door marked "Staff Only." She emerged and strolled over to the desk, a chunky, buxom lady with petite features and a generous smile.

"Hi!" she greeted me.

"Afternoon, ma'am. I'm interested in checking some back issues of the *Denver Post*."

"All righty." Her speech was as Midwestern as a hot pie cooling on a window sill. "Faculty?"

"No, ma'am." I removed my wallet. "I'm Jack LeVine, the private investigator from New York."

Her eyes widened, then twinkled.

"Ooh," she cooed. "Like Sam Spade, or Philip Marlowe. You're one of those fellows?"

"Something like that."

"My, my." She leaned across the desk. "You read Raymond Chandler much, or Hammett?"

"Do you read about libraries?"

She laughed as shrilly as if I had thrust a feather duster beneath her dress.

"I guess I don't, that's true enough. Dear me." She sighed contentedly. "Is this a police matter, Mr. LeVine?"

"It's in connection with a police matter, yes ma'am."

"All righty. I'll write you a pass and you'll present it to Miss Anderson on the second floor." She frowned. "The *Denver Post*," she ruminated. "We'll probably have it. Anything east of the Mississippi, except for *The New York Times*, and you'd be out of luck."

She scribbled on a piece of white paper and handed it to me.

"Miss Anderson will be the gray-haired woman." She lowered her voice confidentially. "Has a slight limp and kind of a bad eye."

"Bad eye?"

"You'll see."

I thanked her and went up the stairs, suddenly very excited about the prospect of reading a sixteen-year-old newspaper.

I was seated at my own table in a small, curtained reading room. The place was empty but for me and the tiny, limping Miss Anderson, who cheerfully insisted on carrying over the half-dozen bound and dusty volumes of the *Denver Post* I had requested.

"Now be very careful with these," she said in a librarian's clear whisper. "Turn the pages slowly and not from the end; turn them down near the spine." She opened a book and demonstrated the correct technique. "The pages will just flake off in your hands otherwise."

"Fine. I'm very much obliged."

"Anything for our lawmen." She smiled behind rimless spectacles. There was a slight milkiness to her left eye. "If you need anything, I'm outside behind the desk. If you can't find me there, try the staff room."

"Again, thanks so much."

She nodded, turned, and padded from the room on rubber-soled shoes. When she closed the door behind her, the room's silence deepened; the only noise was the sleepy drone of an electric fan. That and the hush of turning pages as I began my search for the rapist Pardee.

It took me nearly an hour to go through January. For one thing, I made the error of combing every item, no matter how patently trivial; for another, I got predictably enveloped in 1931 nostalgia, checking on prices, on clothing and automobile styles, on movie and radio listings. I couldn't help myself, with the result that I wasted over an hour in an uneventful month.

February and March went by more quickly, but no more profitably. Still no Pardee. My eyes had begun to hurt and I was dying for a smoke, so I arose, stretched, and went out to the stairwell. I drank some water, sat down on the steps, and puffed a Lucky. It was easy to recall the boredom that drove me out of college.

I returned to my desk at a quarter to four and started leafing through April. The musty smell of the pages and the sunlight beating through the windows was making me drowsy; despite Miss Anderson's strictures, I began turning the pages more quickly, impatient for results.

April passed with nothing more meaningful than the start of the baseball season and predictions that the Athletics had a lock on the American League race. May began with a zoning dispute and a five-car pileup on the interstate. But suddenly, on May 8, my story loomed before me.

And what a story.

The headline read "MAN HELD ON RAPE CHARGE" and beneath it was a grainy two-column photograph of the accused being led into the police station. The caption read "James W. Pardee, 25, of Sedalia, entering police headquarters last night."

He was younger then, and angrier, but there was no mistaking Pardee's face.

I knew him as Johnny Parker.

> Denver police last night arrested James W. Pardee, 25, of Sedalia, charging him with the rape of a Central High School student last Thursday night. Pardee was apprehended in the Big Horn Diner on West Street.
>
> Arresting officers G. A. Charles and C. D. White said they had identified the suspect from a description given by the sixteen-year-old victim. The police are now awaiting positive identification.
>
> Pardee's arrest on the rape charge is his second arrest, according to Denver authorities. He was charged with disturbing the peace during a New Year's celebration at the Big Sky Club in 1927. The charge was dismissed.

I read the story three times. Maybe "read" is the wrong word; I gazed at the newspaper page like a gypsy hag hunched over steaming tea leaves in a carnival tent. I attempted to divine an omen, to conjure a vision out of this fragment of 1931 Denver. Parker's face? Sullen, stunned, but nothing unusual. An arm was guiding Parker into the station house. Officer G. A. Charles? Officer C. D. White?

Clarence White?

That was the big one, the lever to pry open this huge gray clam of a case. If C. D. White, Denver bull, was Clarence White, the FBI's master Red-hound now imbedded in the leftist Hollywood community, then I was clearly open for business. If true it explained a great many things and suggested even more. White the FBI man knew of Parker's background in Denver and used that knowledge to make the studio executive lean on Communist writers, spill to the House Committee, and make trouble for Walter Adrian. Larry Goldmark had told me that Parker used to be friendly with Adrian, Wohl and other "progressive" scenario writers: what had happened to make him shy away? The arrival of C. D. White in Hollywood?

And Dale Carpenter, racing to Parker's house with a folder and greeted at the door like a carrier of typhoid, then mysteriously murdered, his house torn apart. By White? And who was White? Could he have infiltrated so brilliantly that he was among the group of mourners congregated at Walter's house the night of the "suicide"?

All my theorizing, of course, hinged on the identity and whereabouts of C. D. White. If, in fact, he was the FBI undercover man, I could be on the verge of exploding the case. If, on the other hand, C. D. White was still swinging his stick on a Denver beat, all I had was a long and bloody shaggy dog story.

The obvious move was to place another call to Denver. I left the reading room, proffered the bound volumes and my effusive thanks to Miss Anderson, and descended to the library basement, where a pair of empty phone booths were keeping company with a coffee machine. I made the mistake of trying the coffee—a thin brown gruel with specks of curdled milk spinning on its surface—before obtaining a line to Denver police headquarters.

A young woman answered. I asked her where I could get some information about a past member of the Denver force.

"That's Personnel," she told me, pulling the plug.

Personnel picked up. An older woman, she courteously answered my query about C. D. White by announcing that such information could not be given out over the phone.

"I don't want a dossier on White, I just want to know if he's currently a member of the force."

"I'm very sorry, but we cannot transmit such information over the phone."

I gripped the receiver until my hand hurt. If she didn't spill, I'd be forced to go to Denver.

"Ma'am, you're speaking to Lieutenant George Wynn of the Los Angeles Police Department homicide squad. Are you telling me that I have to take a full day out of an important murder investigation," I brought my voice up to a shout, "to find out whether or not C. D. White is currently a member of the Denver police?"

Personnel turned a bit timid.

"What is your name again?"

"Lieutenant Wynn, George Wynn. You want to look it up, fine, but God help the next Denver cop who asks me for a break."

I heard her rifling through a book.

"Oh, yes," she said cheerfully, "here it is: Lieutenant George Wynn, LAPD."

"This is long distance, ma'am."

"Of course. You wanted to know about whom again? I'm afraid I . . ."

"C. D. White. As in Sox."

"It'll take a minute, Lieutenant."

I fed six more quarters into the phone while a brunette knockout in a low-cut sweater dropped her nickel into the coffee dispenser. She bent over to pull out the cup, affording me an unobstructed look at her remarkable nineteen-year-old breasts. When the girl stood upright, they bounced firmly back into place. She caught me gawking and drew her mouth into a thin line of contempt.

"Lieutenant Wynn?"

"Yes, I'm holding on."

"According to my card, C. D. White is no longer a member of the force. He left in 1940."

"Does the card say where he went?"

"No. All I have is that he left voluntarily in 1940."

"I see. And the initials stand for what again?"

"Clarence Depew."

"Thank you very much."

"You're welcome, Lieutenant. You understand, of course, why I hesitated to give the information out immediately. We have regulations, as I'm sure you do in Los Angeles."

"Of course. Thanks again."

I hung up in a high flush of success. Clarence Depew White was my man. I was sure of it, like a bloodhound with a shoe locked in his drooling jaws.

An hour later I sat having Twining's English Breakfast tea in Helen's kitchen with the redhead herself, the sour and edgy Wohls, and Larry Goldmark, who had dropped by to leave off some manuscripts of Walter's and a check from Warner Brothers.

"What do the police make of Dale's murder, Mr. LeVine?" asked Rachel Wohl. Her eyes looked as though they had been left out in the sun and she wouldn't have been much paler if she had died. Her manner, however, remained forceful.

"They're pretty lost, I think."

"You have any theories, Jack?" asked Goldmark. The agent was chewing gum and smoking.

I shrugged. "Theories are cheap. I'm only concerned with Carpenter's death as it relates to Walter's."

"You think it relates?" asked Milton Wohl.

"You don't?" I snapped. The words had come out a little harsher than I had intended. Wohl winced and his wife came bounding to his defense.

"Don't cross-examine Milton, Mr. LeVine. He's gone through enough anguish without being treated in this police-station manner."

Now Helen came out of the bullpen for me.

"Rachel, I don't believe Jack is cross-examining Milt; he's just trying to get at the truth of all this."

The wifely tone of Helen's remarks was lost on no one. Goldmark inhaled enough smoke to fill a zeppelin and shot me a sly, somewhat sickening, glance.

"You think that Carpenter's death makes it unlikely that Walter killed himself?" the agent asked.

"Absolutely," I told him.

"I see," he said, but didn't. "Why?"

I shook my head.

"You'll have to take my word for it, but suicide appears to be out of the question."

Rachel Wohl eyed Helen.

"Has he told you this before?" she demanded. "You knew this before?"

Helen nodded.

"Then why not tell us?" The screenwriter's wife got shrill and anxious. "For God's sake, we can't be trusted? There's some nut loose killing progressives and Milt and I aren't told? We're supposed to go about our business and if someone wants to shoot us through the heart . . ."

"Honey," Wohl said a little sheepishly.

"No, don't stop me, Milt," she continued. Wohl shrugged and looked into his tea. "I'm deeply hurt. That information of literally a life and death nature is kept from us . . . the only justification could be that we are prime suspects. A husband and wife murder team."

"Rachel, I don't think anybody . . ." Goldmark began.

"What does the detective say?" Mrs. Wohl stared at me with those red, frightened eyes.

"I don't blame you for being upset, Mrs. Wohl," I said in my best bedside manner. "But please understand that you and your husband are not 'prime suspects' or anything of that sort."

Milton Wohl looked up from the table, his eyes magnified and dreamy behind the thick lenses.

"I understand that, LeVine," he said softly.

"But the danger?" said his wife. "Leaving us exposed . . ."

"You're in no danger," I assured her. "Unless you know something you're not telling me."

"Like what?" asked Goldmark.

I shook my head.

"That's what I'd like to know." I was being coy, of course, but there was no reason to share what I had learned about Parker and White. "It seems to me, however, that Carpenter was killed over a matter of knowledge. As for Walter, I have to assume the same, but I don't have a shred of evidence to support it."

"But you're sure of it?" asked Goldmark.

"Yep."

The slender agent poured himself some more tea.

"Why?"

"Because there's no other reason for him to have been murdered."

Helen had been staring off into the garden, a fork pressed contemplatively to her lips. She turned to me.

"Unless it was a mistake," she said coolly. "What I mean is that someone thought Walter knew something that he didn't know, or thought he was going to do something that he wasn't going to do. Or just thought that he was someone else."

She put the fork down and lit up an Old Gold, all eyes upon her. Especially mine. Maybe the lady had hit a bull's-eye; it was possible that the uncertainty, the nagging lack of clarity, in Walter's death, could be explained by something as simple as a mistake.

"What do you think about that, Jack?" Helen said to me and me alone. There was a small light of triumph in her eyes and a note of relief in her voice. If Walter's end had resulted from a slip-up, the dense and suspicious air she had been breathing would certainly be lightened and purified.

159

"I think you might be right," I told her.

The Wohls and Goldmark were by now thoroughly confused, but the hell with them. They'd find out sooner or later, if they didn't know now—and their ignorance was a matter of conjecture. I got up and walked over to the window. A couple of jays were having a confused brawl; it ended after a five-second flurry of blue and feathers. I turned and leaned against the sink.

"I'd like to ask you folks just one question," I began, scratching my cheek. "How long have you all been out here?"

Goldmark lit himself another cigarette.

"Living, working?" he asked.

"Both."

"I've been here since '32," said Wohl. "With Rachel. My first screen credit was in '33. *Night Stop.*"

"I remember it," I told Wohl. "About the bus that breaks down."

The writer beamed.

"That's right! Jesus Christ, I didn't think anyone remembered that one. The studio certainly doesn't."

"I saw them all, good and bad. Goldmark, when did you come out here?" I sounded as genial as the host of a quiz program.

"1937," the agent said.

"From where?"

"Pittsburgh. I was a press agent for KDKA radio and they really had me running my butt off. The money wasn't bad but it was Pittsburgh and even when it's sunny all you see is black smoke. Gets to you."

"I'll bet. Then what?"

"Then I came straight out here and hooked up with the Morris office—the William Morris Agency. That was in July of '37. During the war I worked for the Information Office, and opened my own shop after V-J Day."

"Larry's represented me since '39," said Wohl.

Rachel Wohl nodded.

"I remember," she said. "It was about the time of the Nazi–Soviet Pact."

"No connection, I hope," I said pleasantly.

Goldmark guffawed, but the Wohls did not find the remark amusing. Helen covered her smile with a napkin.

"The rest of your group," I continued. "How long have they been here?"

"What do you mean, 'group'?" Rachel Wohl asked coldly.

"Political group."

"How does he know everything?" Mrs. Wohl demanded of Helen. She was furious, shaking.

"Rachel, for God's sake." Wohl got up and walked with her to the far side of the kitchen. "Excuse us," he said over his shoulder.

Goldmark got up and came over to me.

"You think it was one of them?" he asked in a whisper, his face mere cologne-scented inches from mine.

"One of the Wohls?"

"No, not them necessarily. One of the group."

I shrugged, all plodding professional ignorance.

"Who knows? I'm just trying to get an idea of the field."

The agent's eyes narrowed.

"I thought you knew that a long time ago."

"Hell no. My knowledge is pretty limited."

"I figured you were right on top of it, Jack." Now he was beginning to rag me. "Way ahead of the cops."

"Nope," I said amiably. "You overestimate me."

The Wohls returned to the table and sat down. Rachel Wohl blew her nose and wiped at her shining eyes.

"I really don't want to cause any more pain," I told all of them. "But your group, Milt, everybody's been around since 1932 or thereabouts?"

Wohl frowned and drummed his fingers on the arm of his chair. He stared at the ceiling.

"Since '32," he mumbled.

"Take your time," I told him, walking to the refrigerator. I pulled out a bottle of club soda and poured myself half a glass.

"No," Wohl finally said. "I'll tell you, LeVine. Carroll Arthur has been in Hollywood since the twenties and he started coming around in, say, '36. But are you interested in the length of political activity or how long they've been in Hollywood?"

"The politics is secondary. Helpful but secondary. Don't tell me any more about the politics than you want to; I understand your position right now."

Wohl shot a sharp glance at Goldmark, who snuffed out his cigarette and lit another. Everyone was just electric with anxiety.

"I appreciate that, LeVine," Wohl said. He played with the remains of a pastry on the plate before him. "Carroll Arthur, late twenties, like I said. Sig Friedland is an Austrian refugee. He lived in England for a couple of years and made his way here in . . . 1941." He looked to his wife. "Was it '41?"

She nodded.

" '41, early '42 the latest."

"Fine," I said. "Go on, Milt."

"Now Dale Carpenter had been out here since the thirties," the writer continued, "but his political involvement dates from the early forties."

"Since the invasion," said Mrs. Wohl.

"Which invasion?" I asked.

"Since Hitler invaded the Soviet Union," Wohl told me. "The Nazi–Soviet Pact was a pragmatic, time-saving move, of course, but at the time it caused an uproar in the progressive community. A great many people dropped out; almost no one joined up."

"But things livened up when the Germans went galloping into Russia?" I asked.

"Sure." Wohl relaxed a bit, happy to be discussing history rather than murder—a fine distinction at best. "See, people realized that Stalin had only been buying time. With the Allies dawdling over the establishment of a second front, seemingly content to let the Soviets absorb enormous losses . . . well, the Nazi–Soviet Pact, in retrospect, made a whale of a lot of sense. People woke up."

"Henry made a big difference at that point," Mrs. Wohl interjected.

"Absolutely. When Henry came in it gave us a big boost," Wohl agreed.

"You're talking about Henry Perillo?" I asked.

"That's right," said Wohl. "Henry not only possessed a great deal of theoretical knowledge, but he had great practical know-how in terms of organizing. His union background was invaluable."

I resumed my seat.

"But you belong to a union, too, right?" I asked.

Wohl smiled.

"There's a great deal of difference between the Writers' Guild and the craft unions. We're still babes in the woods."

"Not quite," said Goldmark.

"In any case," I said, steering the conversation back to where I wanted it, "Perillo came late to Hollywood?"

"Sometime during the war, Hon?" the writer asked his wife. " '43, '44?"

"Late '43," said Mrs. Wohl.

"Uh-huh," I said matter of factly. "You have any idea where he was before?"

The Wohls searched each other's faces and came up empty.

"Wasn't it Denver?" asked Goldmark. "I vaguely remember something about Denver."

Rachel Wohl, teacup at her lip, nodded emphatically.

"You're right. Larry's right, Milt. He had been active in union-organizing in Denver."

"So he was in Denver until '43?" I asked.

"I don't believe so," said Wohl. "He'd been traveling. But that goes into areas he'd have to discuss himself."

"Of course," I assured him. "But you say he galvanized your group when he got here?"

"Definitely," said Mrs. Wohl. "He broadened our scope, was heavily involved in the Popular Front move, but always had a clear sense of the ultimate goal we all were shooting for: a world of economic justice."

"You'd say he was the leader?" I asked.

"We have no leaders, Mr. LeVine," Wohl said quietly, but with some force. "Henry helped us clarify our thinking."

"And despite his relatively late arrival, he was accepted wholeheartedly?" I went on. But I had asked one question too many.

Wohl's eyes floated uncertainly. "Do you suspect Henry Perillo of something, Mr. LeVine? If so, I wish you'd come out and say it."

It was time for me to fold my tent and steal across the darkening sands.

"I don't suspect him more than anyone else." I casually lit a Lucky. "It's just that since he was the last to come to Hollywood, his background contains the largest number of unknowns."

Everyone sat pondering the sense, or nonsense, of my words.

"Henry is beyond reproach," said Mrs. Wohl.

I shook my head. "Ma'am, *I'm* not even beyond reproach."

There was some light laughter. Nobody falling into the aisle, just some chuckles and smirks of relief. Helen began clearing the dishes and I was pleased to help her. It cued Goldmark and the Wohls to shuffle their feet and get up.

"Helen, we'll be running," said Wohl.

The redhead turned to her husband's friends.

"What can I say?" she told them. "For looking after me,

for taking the time to baby-sit . . . I'm such awful company, I know."

Wohl kissed her. "Hush," he said affectionately. "You're a dear girl and you're doing remarkably." He looked at me. "What do you think of the courage of this girl, LeVine?"

"She's terrific," I told him.

"See?" Wohl said, almost gaily. "And he's one of those hard-boiled detectives."

"He's not so tough," Helen said with a smile.

Wohl laughed but his wife stared at me with a peculiar mixture of loathing and awe. I held out my hand to her.

"Sorry to have upset you. It certainly wasn't my intention."

"I know," she said without much conviction, then turned and gave Helen a dutiful kiss.

"You going to Zack's tonight?" Goldmark asked Helen.

"Probably," she said.

"Fine. See you there." The agent kissed her.

There was a final chorus of good-byes and be-wells as Helen walked the trio to the front door.

By the time Helen had closed the door and returned to the kitchen, I had gone through her personal directory and come up with Perillo's home address and phone number, copying the digits onto a matchbook.

Helen curled up on the banquette. I leaned against the sink.

"Who's Zack," I asked, "and what's tonight?"

"Zack Gross, the producer. He's having a meeting-party kind of thing, ostensibly to discuss the HUAC developments."

"You going?"

"I'd like to, if you'll come with me."

"I have an errand to run first. What time does it start?"

"Nine. What's the errand?"

"I have to see a guy."

"That's very helpful, Jack." She patted her hand on the banquette. "Sit with me for a minute."

I did so and received a hug as my reward.

"How did the police treat you?" Helen asked.

"I didn't lose any teeth."

"I see," she said evenly. "Are you going to tell me anything?" Helen was getting annoyed and I couldn't really blame her, but while the case was at such a delicate point, it seemed foolish to load her with details. They would only make her jumpy.

"I think I'm on to something, but I've got to work it out. Trust me."

"It's not a matter of trust, Jack. I just don't enjoy ignorance. It's dangerous."

"So's knowledge."

"Oh Jack, come on, let's not play word games."

"All right. What specifically do you want to know?"

"What do the police think?"

"They don't think. Their hands are tied on this one. The FBI is running the show."

Her eyes grew big, that wonderful jaw dropped just a trifle.

"Really? The FBI?"

"Really. An FBI man named Clarence White is in charge. Ever hear of him?"

She shook her head.

"No."

"That's what I thought. Now I've really got to blow."

Helen wrapped her arms about my chest and squeezed. "One more minute, Jack."

She slid up on the banquette and kissed me, lightly. Then with a little more force, nibbling on my bottom lip.

"I still have thirty seconds," she whispered.

She pressed closer to me and my brain began passing all the appropriate signals down the line. The green lights began flashing, the vat began bubbling. But LeVine is a dutiful fellow.

"Time's up," I said, disengaging myself with a final peck

on her broad brow. "I can assure you that I don't want to go, but it's important."

"Cock-teaser," she said with a grin. "You'll pick me up at 8:30 or so?"

"I'll try, but if you don't hear from me by, say, 8:15, go with the Wohls and I'll meet you there. What's Gross' address?"

"Number 384 St. Cloud. It's in Bel Air."

"That's very fancy?"

"You won't believe how fancy. Incredible. Gross married money and made a lot on his own; he's produced a lot of biggies."

"But he's political."

"Carefully so. A good liberal type."

She got up and walked me out to the hall. I took my hat out of the closet.

"As ever, don't let anyone in you don't recognize," I told her.

Helen leaned by the door; a teen-aged girl saying goodnight to a study date.

"You won't tell me where you're going?"

"Not to worry."

She looked into my eyes and suddenly all traces of the teen-ager vanished; the widow, seeking revenge, reappeared.

"Do you suspect Henry Perillo, Jack?"

What the hell.

"Yes I do."

She looked down at the floor, arms folded, and let her system absorb the news. Then she looked up, composed and even.

"He'll be at that party tonight," she said.

"That's okay. If you feel you can't talk to him without developing a tic, then duck him."

She compressed that beautiful mouth.

"You really think it's Henry? I just can't believe it."

"I have suspicions, but nothing substantial. Okay?"

"Okay."

She opened the door for me.

"Try and be back soon, Jack. I'd like to go to Zack's with you."

"I'll try. Listen to the radio, relax."

"You just take care of yourself."

We kissed and then I left the house. She stood in the doorway and I turned to wave good-bye. We waved for a long moment, reluctant to part.

I think we both knew what we were in for.

erillo lived at 3410 The Paseo, in L.A.'s Highland Park district, a pleasantly scruffy working-class neighborhood of mongrel dogs, rust-brown children, and amiable Mexicans repairing and scrubbing their 1936 Fords. I arrived at seven and it seemed that everyone had just completed supper: dishes were being scraped and the porches and yards were filling up with racing kids and mutts. A guitar was being strummed melodically and laughter fell like light rain. It was an unlikely turf to stalk someone I thought guilty of murder, an unlikely turf to do anything but have a few beers and welcome the night.

The Paseo was a short residential street that ran a few blocks and ended on a weed-covered hill. I drove past Perillo's house very slowly; the driveway and curb were empty, but the house was positioned too high up for me to see if the lights were on or off. So I continued on past the house, turned back down to Verdugo Road, and stopped in at a tavern called El Sombrero.

The Sombrero was as dark and quiet as if it had closed. Two gentlemen were either sleeping or praying at the bar; the moon-faced Mexican bartender was seated on a stool, reading a scratch sheet and chewing contemplatively on a beef jerky. I ordered a draft and asked if the phone was working.

"Only if you put a nickel in," he joked in softly accented English.

I walked to the back and called Perillo's home. His phone rang a dozen times before I hung up and sauntered back to the bar. My beer was waiting. I was parched and the brew went down in three swallows.

"This place liven up on weekends?" I asked the bartender.

"Un cementerio, a cemetery. One good horse," he snapped his fingers, "and you watch my ass go out the door. Sit here all day, talk to the flies." He whirled an index finger about his temple. "Go *completamente loco."*

"My office is like that sometimes. In New York. Just me and the dust."

"Then we're both *loco,"* he told me and smiled.

One of the men at the bar woke up and promptly fell off his stool.

"Madre de Dios," said the bartender, getting up to help.

I parked the Chrysler on Thirty-fifth Avenue, an uphill street that dead-ended into The Paseo, and began walking up to Perillo's house. It was past dusk now and the brown and white faces arrayed on the porches regarded me with mild curiosity. A few folks nodded in greeting and I returned the favor. They were no more suspicious of me than I of them, yet a person traveling on foot anywhere in Los Angeles was to be viewed as a pleasant oddity, an amusement of the evening.

By the time I reached Number 3410 I was slightly out of breath—and I was still only half-way to Perillo's house. The smallish cottage was perched on a plot located about fifty yards up a steep hill studded with avocado and palm trees. Cracked stone slabs, sprouting hardy weeds and wildflowers, served as a roundabout staircase to the top, but a pick and rope would have been appropriate. It was the perfect setting for someone who wished to discourage visitors, or wanted a long look at them before they got to the door.

I climbed the stairs. The evening air was damp and my shirt was pretty well soaked when I reached the top. I mopped my brow with a hanky and rang Perillo's bell, twice. When no one answered, I tried the door and was not surprised to find it locked.

So I walked around to the back, where I would be safely out of view, Perillo's neighbors being vacant lots. The back contained a small, unkempt yard, perhaps four hundred square feet of brown and dusty grass. In its center stood a rusted, sagging swing and seesaw apparatus, looking as ancient and splay-footed as the skeleton of an infant dinosaur. I didn't figure Perillo to use the swing with any regularity at all. There were some fruit trees and beneath them sweet, rotten droppings of oranges and avocados. Two metal chairs faced each other beneath the trees, their seats shiny with stagnant water.

A few bright stars had appeared and the crickets and katydids had begun their electric evening music. I walked toward the rear of the house and found another door. Another locked door. I tried a few old hotel keys, but I could have used my pecker for all the good they did. Perspiring like a Sicilian road-builder, I continued my stealthy, counterclockwise encirclement of the house, finally coming upon a locked but flimsy window. It could be raised about an inch and a half above the sill, and that was all I really needed. I hunted down a fallen tree limb and jammed it into the window as a wedge, then pressed down hard upon it. The lock loosened but didn't give. Awash with sweat, I leaned against the tree limb with my full weight. The lock buckled and broke, the window flew upward, and I fell down upon a half-dozen mushy avocados.

I tossed the tree limb back where I had found it and climbed into a small and musty room, a bedroom, then shut the window and returned the lock so that it appeared to be in place.

The bedroom was sparsely furnished, neat, and looked rarely used. There was a single bed, a night stand and lamp, a battered chest of drawers, a canvas chair, and bookshelves constructed of varnished pine boards. The books—complete works of Marx and Engels, volumes by Michael Bakunin, Karl Liebknecht, Rosa Luxemburg, Karl Kautsky, Eduard Bernstein, by Americans like William Z. Foster, Michael Gold, and John Howard Lawson—were arranged alphabetically. Very few of them looked to have been read; the pages were white and unsmudged, the bindings still cracked.

I went through the chest of drawers, quickly and lightly of hand, coming up empty. Perillo favored white socks, white boxer shorts, and white short-sleeved shirts. There was a jar of pennies in one drawer, a cigar box full of tie clips and cuff links—uninscribed, unmarked, and uninteresting—in another. The taste and style were those of a man with twenty years at the Bureau of Motor Vehicles beneath his belt.

I opened a closet. Two brown sports jackets hung in dank silence and back issues of *The New Masses* had been piled in a rear corner, making room for the Perillo shoe collection, basic black with airholes. A damp pair of workboots attracted my attention; I picked them up and observed that the soles were lightly breaded with sand. I put the boots back down, remembering Santa Monica and two bored thugs waiting for their boss. Then I headed for the living room.

It was down a brief, blank hallway and was dominated by two huge portraits of Lenin and Stalin, staring at each other across an ersatz fireplace. Mustachioed Stalin had been given the beatific smile and polished cheeks of a people's saint, while bearded Lenin exhibited the fierce and messianic urgency of the true believer. They loomed like godheads over a living room furnished in the scuffed and orphaned style of the Salvation Army: a yellow convertible sofa, an "easy" chair, a rocking chair, a glass-topped coffee table, a shovel and iron for the nonexistent fireplace, and a throw rug. That was it. I looked through the cushions of the sofa but searching this near-vacant room was as pointless as it was simple.

Then there was a study, the only room in the joint with the clutter commonly associated with human habitation. It was more an alcove, really, six by eight or so, located off the "dining room" (a bridge table) and fashioned into a separate room by the installation of sliding doors. Perillo, after all, was a carpenter.

I entered the study and went straight to a column of wooden file drawers, unmarked and brass-handled. They stood across from a small desk on which a Remington typewriter stood uncovered. It occurred to me to take a sample off the typewriter and I reached for a sheet of paper.

Which is when I heard the footsteps.

Someone was coming up the stairs; there was no mistaking the methodical beat of shoe on stone. I backed out of the study and went to the living room, which had a window that faced front. The steps grew more distinct, stopped for the pause to catch breath, then resumed. I watched, tense and fascinated, as the top bristles of Henry Perillo's crewcut came into view. For a few seconds I stood cemented to the floor, but as he slowly came around the next-to-last "S" curve and his forehead appeared, I dashed to the bedroom and crawled beneath the bed, like any other schmuck caught in the right place at the wrong time.

Getting beneath the bed was not as easy as it looked. The frame was close to the dusty floor and it was a single, which didn't leave much slack space for someone six feet, two hundred pounds in size. Someone like me, for instance. Add to that the fact that the bedspread did not reach to the floor, despite my tugging, and I was all too visible.

I heard Perillo unlock the front door and enter. He was whistling the Marine Corps Hymn, an odd selection, I thought, and no particular favorite of Stalin's. Water began running in the bathroom: Perillo gargled and rinsed, then shut the faucet off. His footsteps clattered on the kitchen linoleum. He blew his nose. He opened the refrigerator door, closed it, then uncapped a bottle. From the nearly inaudible hiss that followed the pouring of the bottle's contents into a glass, the trained LeVine ear determined that Perillo was having himself a beer. Flat on my back, surrounded by tufted swirls of hair and dust, the sound of the gushing cold brew forced me to swallow reflexively.

While I lay there contemplating my need for a Blatz, Perillo went into the study and began typing. I listened to his careful pecking; he was a two-finger man. After a few minutes, his telephone rang. It rang twice, then stopped. It rang once again, and stopped. When it rang again, Perillo instantly picked up. His words were music to my ears.

"White. Yes, Chuck, I'm typing the report up now. . . . In a half-hour or so, maybe less. Probably less, in fact . . . yes . . . I'll be leaving for the studio as soon as I finish, so figure an hour from now should be about right . . . check . . . fine . . . yes, the ring is tightening and I think we've got them on the run . . . right."

Clarence Depew White, alias Henry Perillo, hung up and resumed typing, while I commenced thinking about possible ways to get out of the house before he did. It was an awkward problem because the house was so small; any noise would get the FBI man flying out of his chair. I could always wait until he left and then drive furiously over to Warner Brothers, assuming that was the "studio" he was talking about "leaving for." But if another studio was involved, then I would have blown two unique opportunities: to observe White's modus operandi and to gain access to the memo he was typing at that very moment. I fully intended to glom that vital piece of paper by any means save murder.

So I had to make a break for it, as cautious and circumspect a break as I could fashion. No fireworks, no heroics; just a mild-mannered attempt at leaving the house without getting my throat slit.

I removed my Colt and began wiggling sideways, like an aging belly dancer, slowly and without much rhythm, cutting a broad swath through the dust. Proceeding at an arthritic pace, I managed to shimmy from beneath the bed in just under five minutes. The typewriter clacked away uninterrupted, reassuring background music to my planned exit.

I arose from the floor very delicately, a prima ballerina doing "Sleeping Beauty" before a packed house, and started quietly toward the window. A fly hummed past my nose, but I stoically withheld the potentially fatal sneeze. I reached the window, easily removed the broken lock, and grasped the twin handles attached to the white moulding.

White stopped typing.

I froze, freedom before me, and waited for the typewriter to resume. When it didn't, I returned the lock, stepped from the window, and ducked down beside the bed, where I said my rosary and held my bad breath. White's ill-oiled chair shrieked as he got up, then I heard the FBI undercover agent yawn.

He walked into the bathroom and pissed up a storm, leaving the door open, as one does when alone. He stopped pissing. I heard the short metallic buzz of a closing zipper, then White hawked up a mouthful and spat into the standing urine. He flushed the toilet. Each sound echoed like thunder through the empty house.

White strolled into the kitchen and pulled another beer from the igloo, then returned to the study. I listened for his chair to creak. It did. White coughed and began typing again.

Confidently but carefully, I got to my feet and slipped over to the window. Once more I removed the lock and gripped the handles on the frame. I pulled upwards. The window arose as easily and silently as smoke but, its lock ruined, would not stay up by itself. So, one hand pressed flat against the raised frame, I extended my leg out over the sill, saw my pants leg impaled upon a nail for a panicky eternity of three seconds, and vaulted outside.

I let the window drop nice and easy and ducked down against the house, protected by the darkness. I sighed and felt a queasy chill as the evening air met my sweat-soaked clothes, then crouched away from the house, standing up as I crossed over the warped and swaybacked fence that separated Perillo's grounds from the bordering lot.

Stumbling over rocks, I bounded down the hill at an awkward trot, gathering speed as I reached the bottom, landing on the street with the breathless grace of a kid in mid-Saturday romp. A dog and a chicken, wandering up The Paseo, watched me with polite interest. I told them I thought the Adrian case was finally coming to a head. The dog wagged his tail, but I don't think the chicken knew what the hell I was talking about.

Clarence White came out of the house fifteen minutes later and quickly descended the winding steps. I was seated in the Chrysler, watching his house from the rear-view mirror and nervously blowing a Lucky. Could he leave the house without my seeing? Was there a hidden garage, a second car?

But no, here he was, brown-suited and white-shirted, looking up and down the street before entering and starting his car, a blue Nash. I slid down in my seat as he rolled slowly down Thirty-fifth Avenue, and didn't even turn the ignition key until the FBI man had come to a full stop and turned right onto Verdugo.

I tried to stay way back of him in the sparse nighttime traffic, but it wasn't easy: White rarely went over forty-five and drove as erratically as a hophead in a Coney Island bumper car. He switched lanes, braked for no apparent reason, slowed near green lights and sailed absent-mindedly through red ones. I began to fear that he might have picked me up; a man who did undercover work was apt to suspect he was being followed while taking his morning crap. Add his police experience and you had a person with all the professional tools to discover and lose a tail in a matter of minutes.

When the Nash turned down Barham Boulevard, twenty frustrating minutes later, I knew that unless White was decoying me, he was headed for the Warners lot. Traffic was extremely thin and I did not wish to be discovered at this late stage of the game, so I pulled into a drive-in called Mister Taco, on Cahuenga, and let him get out of range.

A slim high-school girl in a sombrero, white silk blouse, and black pants came to the car and asked what I was having.

"I'm waiting for a friend," I told her.

"You can't wait here."

"Why not?"

The girl shrugged in the direction of a small, dark man working behind the counter.

"It's his rule."

"That Mister Taco himself?"

She lowered her head and managed a shy smile.

"No-oooo, silly. He's just the manager."

"And he doesn't like guys hanging around."

"It's mainly for school kids, the rule. They stay till closing otherwise. You could just order a Coke."

"Fine. A small Coke." I handed the girl a quarter. "No ice in that, and no Coke. And forget about the cup and keep the change."

She pocketed the quarter and grinned.

"You're pretty neat," she told me.

"I'll come by next year and give you another quarter. Consider it a fixed income."

A stripped-down prewar Chevvy roared in beside us and began honking. The girl in the sombrero turned and squealed in delight as a half-dozen young boys leaned out the windows. California was another planet altogether. I backed out of Mister Taco and drove straight to Warner Brothers.

There was a little trouble at the main gate, involving the exact purpose of my visit. It took a few minutes of heated explanation—investigating Adrian's death, New York City detective, urgent, you have any questions call Parker—to gain admission to the lot. The irritable, gray-haired gateman finally waved me through with a final "next time you'll have to bring a signed permit." I barreled up the main drag, headlights off, and parked the Chrysler between a bulldozer and the north wall of the commissary, safely out of sight.

Then I headed for the Western Street.

Call it instinct, sixth sense, or a bloodhound's red-eyed judgment, but if White wasn't in the vicinity of that fantasy frontier village, then I'd hang up the gumshoes and go into the junior sportswear line. All the activity in the Adrian case that centered around the Warners lot—Walter's murder and the attempt on my life—had occurred on the Western Street. More particularly, it had occurred in the narrow area defined by the gallows and the jailhouse. If Clarence White was on the lot, the odds seemed very good that he'd be operating in that vicinity.

I cut back to the frontier town through the friendly white houses of Small-Town America, and crept up to the back entrance of the saloon. The room was empty. On tip-toe, hand on gun, I entered the saloon and slipped along the wall until I could peek over the tops of the swinging doors.

The blue Nash was parked across the street, in front of the jailhouse.

I congratulated myself and waited, wondering whether

it might make sense to rush over and surprise White. But surprise him doing what? As Perillo, he worked at Warners. He had excuses for being here. I didn't.

A minute or two into my vacillating, White stepped from the dark jailhouse and cast a long, anxious look around before shutting the door. I flattened myself against the saloon wall and listened as he started the Nash and drove hurriedly away.

I poked my head out the swinging doors and saw the sheets of dust rising as the Nash disappeared from view. I stood my ground for a minute or two, eyes darting from street to watch, until I convinced myself that White had actually driven away and was not hovering outside with an ice pick clenched in his fist. I pushed the doors open and raced across the empty street, gun drawn, every bit as relaxed as a circus aerialist with hemorrhoids.

The jailhouse door opened with a horror-matinee creak. I cautiously stepped through the low, narrow doorway and immediately kicked over a brass spittoon; it rolled noisily to the far side of the room before smacking into the wooden wall. I listened attentively to its diminishing vibrations, feeling the slightest bit foolish, then finally pocketed my Colt and whipped out a pencil flashlight.

I scanned the room with the concentrated beam. The jailhouse was in good repair, with a minimum of candy wrappers and technical debris on the wooden floor. There was a set of jail cells, a large rolltop desk over which hung the Gilbert Stuart portrait of George Washington, a table and chairs, a pot-bellied stove, and a hat rack. The room was damp and chilly; in darkness, one might have thought he was wandering about a cave.

My watch read eight-fifteen. White had told his telephone contact to "figure an hour from now" at seven-thirty; the person or persons would be arriving in fifteen minutes or so, presumably to pick up the typed memorandum. I didn't have any time at all and began going through the room like a dervish, checking off the most obvious spots for concealment: within the stove, behind the Washington portrait, inside the desk drawers, beneath the bunks in the jail cells. It took only five minutes but I came up with nothing, and even for five minutes' work that's not much.

The next strategic assault had me tapping against areas of wall, listening for the tell-tale hollow thump of a hidden compartment. Another five minutes vanished and the net result was that my knuckles hurt. Eight-twenty-five. I should have been making my exit but an ambitious brain cell suddenly dropped before my eyes a card reading, Hey putz, White's a carpenter. The only substantial wooden piece in the room was the desk. I sped over to where it stood and dove for the floor.

Flat on my back in the hollow between the two sets of drawers, I scrutinized the inside boards for the sign of a sliding panel. Nothing. I went lower, twisting so that I was virtually imprisoned in the well of the desk. I tapped, clawed, and tugged, when, with jewel box precision, a section of the base came loose, revealing a small knob. I pulled at it and a shallow drawer—just big enough for, say, a manila folder—came out in my hand. Inside was a plain white envelope and inside the envelope a pink memorandum bearing the letterhead of the Federal Bureau of Investigation. I slipped the envelope into my inside jacket pocket, wrenched myself from beneath the desk, and went to the door.

I leaned my damp and glistening skull into the night air. The street was as dead as a landlord's heart. I went outside, shutting the door behind me, and walked back toward the saloon. As I reached the far side of the street, the drone of an approaching car became audible. And more audible. The glare of headlights swept across the ghostly storefronts as a dark sedan turned the corner and came down the street.

Standing just inside the saloon, I watched as the car, a Plymouth, braked sharply across the way. Two men in raincoats, their fedoras brim-down, jumped out of the car and ran inside the jailhouse. I stared intently at the two figures but for all I could see in the darkness, they could have been Amos 'n Andy.

Since the two beagles would go straight for the desk, whereupon they would be disappointed, confused, and perhaps suspicious, I decided to get off the Warners lot as quickly as possible. I could read the memo somewhere else. So I left as I came, slipping out the back of the saloon, past those cheerful houses of American innocence, and into the camouflaged Chrysler, which I gunned. A sense of urgency and fear possessed me as I streaked off the lot at sixty miles per hour.

Call it instinct.

read the pink FBI memorandum while getting a fill-up at a Texaco station on Barham. I'm not exactly sure how I finished it.

TO: P. J. DAVIS

FROM: CLARENCE WHITE

RE: ROLE OF HELEN ADRIAN AND JACK LEVINE IN
    COMMUNIST ACTION PLAN

It can now be reported that the Communist plan for avoiding prosecution in the murders of Walter Adrian and Dale Carpenter is at hand. Once again the insidious cunning of the Soviets is obvious; the entire matter has been brilliantly conceived and executed.

Be assured that the undercover unit is well aware of the dimensions and strategy of the case and is on top of all aspects. THE LOS ANGELES POLICE ARE TO DO NOTHING! THEIR INTERFERENCE AT THIS CRITICAL POINT WOULD BE FATAL!

The facts of the matter are as follows:

1. Walter Adrian and Dale Carpenter were killed by none other than "Helen Adrian," in reality a Soviet national named VERA DROSHDEKOVYA, whose marriage to screenwriter Adrian was planned by the NKVD (Soviet secret police) as a way of gaining a pipeline to the movie colony.

For two years, all went smoothly. "Helen Adrian" filed regular reports on the growth of the Party in Hollywood—while cleverly "refusing" to join herself. She handpicked candidates for espionage.

But when Walter Adrian unknowingly "confided" to his wife, early this year, that he planned to leave the Party and tell the House Committee on Un-American Activities what he knew about Red activities in Hollywood, she reported this knowledge to Moscow and was informed that her husband must be liquidated. A fake "suicide" was planned.

2. To assist her in this plot, New York Party functionary JACOB LEVINE, a "private detective" operating under the name of "Jack LeVine" was summoned West to help "investigate" the death of Adrian. In reality, it was LeVine's job to protect Miss Droshdekovya and create distractions. It is obvious that he has succeeded. It also appears that LeVine and Droshdekovya have become lovers.

3. Dale Carpenter was murdered when he learned that his friend Walter Adrian had not died by his own hand, but had in fact been murdered, and by "Mrs. Adrian." (We have not determined how Carpenter obtained this knowledge.) Not

knowing who to turn to, Carpenter went to the home of Johnny Parker, a friend of the House Committee. He was followed there by LeVine, who informed "Mrs. Adrian" of the development. She went to the movie star's house that evening and, with the deadly accuracy that is the hallmark of Soviet agents, shot him through the heart.

PLAN OF ACTION

Vera Droshdekovya plans to leave Hollywood and return to Moscow, abetted by LeVine. WE ARE TO LET HER LEAVE AND ANNOUNCE THE CARPENTER MATTER UNSOLVED. She will be followed, of course, but not detained. Her activities are of great interest to us. Her imprisonment would cause a sensation, BUT WOULD SEND THE SOVIET ESPIONAGE UNDERGROUND FURTHER UNDERGROUND. They are currently visible and under surveillance.

IN SHORT, MISS DROSHDEKOVYA MUST BE ALLOWED TO "DISAPPEAR."

REPEAT: MISS DROSHDEKOVYA *MUST* BE ALLOWED TO DISAPPEAR.

I was numb when I finished the document. White had found an out and it was both ingenious and fiendish in conception. He would murder Helen and be covered by this memo; in turn, he had incriminated me as a Soviet agent. By the time things got sorted out, if ever, White would be long gone.

"That'll be three dollars," said the grease monkey, tapping me on the shoulder. "Check the oil?"

I threw him three bills and left the station as if a checkered flag had flashed before the windshield, pulling out onto Barham without even checking for traffic. A car screeched to a halt behind me; cursing and honking filled the air. I moved into the left lane, impervious to everything but the fact that I had to get to Helen before Clarence White did.

The Chrysler was a hell of a car and it responded splendidly to my cowboy recklessness behind the wheel, but it still took forty-five agonizing minutes to get to Bel Air. Five or ten of those minutes were spent squinting at street signs as I cruised through Bel Air trying to find 384 St. Cloud amidst the curving roadways and fortress-high shrubbery of this poshest of neighborhoods.

But you'd drive past the Chicago fire before you'd miss the home of Zack Gross. It was what we call a mansion: three stories, pillared, and snow white. Thirty-five rooms, minimum. I expected to see Rhett and Scarlett come dancing out the front door, such was the heady, lanterned aura of the house, cushioned as it was by wide and scented lawns, bordered by exquisite shrubbery that strained against high, spiked fences. The fences looked freshly painted and freshly sharpened.

All three floors of the Gross mansion were lighted and alive; through the windows I observed what had to be a few hundred people standing about and chatting. And among them would be a man known as Henry Perillo, drink in hand, addressing his remarks to the problems of the body politic and the decaying structure of capitalism, remaining genial and modest in manner, keeping his eyes fixed above the shoulders of his immediate social circle, scanning the room for the widow of Walter Adrian. And when he spotted her, he would politely excuse himself from the group, greet Helen effusively, and steer her to a corner, then summon her outside for a serious talk. In that crush of people, who would notice the absence of two people?

I whipped around the long circular driveway and was stopped in front of the house by a gray-haired Negro standing in the road and holding up his hand. He walked over to the car and handed me a numbered ticket.

"Valet parking, sir."

"Do I have a choice?"

"No choice, no charge," he said with a hoarse laugh. "Big party tonight. I got to park 'em or nobody'll get out afterwards."

I stepped from the car and the Negro slid into the driver's seat.

"Go in and enjoy yourself." he said cheerfully. "Don't worry about no Chrysler. I got Rolls cars back to back and no scratches."

"You park a blue Nash recently?"

He regarded me with untroubled brown eyes.

"Blue Nash?" he repeated innocently. "Not sure. Lot of cars tonight, mister. Lot of cars."

I slipped a buck into his hand.

"Yeah," he told me. "Blue Nash. Twenty minutes ago."

"It still here?"

"Far as I know, but I've been back and forth. Nash had an end spot. Man could slip out, if that's what you want to know."

It was and wasn't. I bolted up the front stairs and rang the bell.

A butler opened up, in full soup and fish, poised in front of a curving stairway, his brilliantined hair bright beneath a chandelier.

"No coat," I told him. "Where's the party?"

He asked my name, then turned on his heel and goose-stepped away. Maybe I was supposed to wait but I didn't have the time, so I walked directly behind him and entered a reception room as large and noisy as St. Nick's Arena. Perhaps a hundred people were standing about the room, in full conversational roar, propelled by urgency and drink to discuss the fevered events of the past week. As I pushed my way through the crowd in search of Helen, curious heads turned; fragments of sentences indicated, amazingly enough, that I was recognized.

"Hired by Adrian," I heard. "New York, I don't know if he suspects, . . . school friend. . . ." Other bits of conversation drifted past: "I heard Warner is scared shitless,

186

. . . goddamn Menjou can't wait, . . . it starting in April?
. . . Dalton didn't say but I think so, . . . oil money behind Nixon."

The din was awful, but what a crowd. I was too anxious
to do much gawking, but in my progress across the room
I managed to step on Spencer Tracy's toe, jostle Paulette
Goddard's drink, and rub against Myrna Loy's ass. Katha-
rine Hepburn was with Tracy, her exquisite, sculpted face
looking tired and drained; she was letting Tracy do all the
talking. Cornel Wilde was having an animated conversation with Paul Henreid; Conrad Veidt, looking nothing like
a Nazi officer, had his hand on Henreid's shoulder and
was telling Dorothy McGuire a joke. "Oh, Connie," she
laughed.

In a corner was my own favorite, John Garfield. Trim
and dark, he was nibbling on a sandwich and bending his
ear toward a couple of talkative dolls in very low-cut
dresses. Their combined four tits, at close range, were
Himalayan in snowy grandeur and Garfield couldn't keep
his eyes off them.

It was all pretty fascinating for a Sunnyside schnook like
me, but I would have swapped the lot of them for a glimpse
of Helen or Clarence White.

I wandered through an archway into a smaller area, a
dining room, I think. Two dozen people were milling about
and the decibel level was a good deal lower. Eddie Cantor
was there and he appeared to be boring Ava Gardner, who,
in a blue silk dress slit up to her thigh, was an incitement
to riot. Gloriously alluring, but as soft as a steel boot. She
wandered away from Cantor in mid-sentence to greet
Gregory Peck. Very tall man. I recognized no one else; a
small woman, fifty or so, was drunk and appeared to be
weeping. Her tears aroused my professional curiosity, but
there wasn't any time. No time at all.

Lost, wide-eyed, and increasingly agitated, I went from
room to room, scanning faces, checking off backs of heads.

I picked a glass of champagne off a passing silver tray and downed it in rapid gulps, then headed for the stairs, knocking over Danny Kaye and failing to apologize.

I ran up the stairs. In a small den on the second floor were Milton and Rachel Wohl. They were having an argument with a loud man whom they introduced to me as Jerry Wald.

"Where's Helen?" I asked, without even acknowledging Wald.

The Wohls looked at each other, as if trying to agree on an answer.

"C'mon!" I roared. "Did she come with you? Is she here? Did she leave?"

Rachel Wohl became alarmed and stood up. "Is something the matter?"

"Not yet," I told her. "Where is she?"

"She was sitting with us until about ten minutes ago," said Milton Wohl, puzzled at my outburst. "Then Henry came up and said he wanted to talk . . ."

I turned and ran out of the room.

Henry Fonda was coming up the stairs; I went flying past him.

"Hey, Mister," he said amiably. "Where's the fire?"

The extraordinary brunette on his arm merely giggled. I took the last three steps at a jump, dashed past the butler and out the front door. The door closed behind me and the evening's cool silence made the party seem even more unreal than it was. It roared on dully behind me.

I ran around to the back of the house, where guest cars were being parked on a huge lawn bordering a pair of tennis courts. The Negro was getting out of a Packard and saw me racing toward him.

"Leaving already?" he said with a broad smile. "That Chrysler of yours is kind of wedged in; take me a few minutes to get it out."

Jesus Holy Christ.

"Listen," I asked, knowing the answer, "the Nash still here?"

The Negro put his finger to his nose and rubbed.

"Nope," he finally said. "Left five minutes ago. Maybe ten."

"Man and a woman, a redhead?"

"Yessir."

"In a hurry?"

"Nope. Redhead was drunk, I think."

Drugged.

"Get me my car. Pronto."

"It'll take a while, Mister. Like I said, she's wedged in."

A sense of futility and anguish possessed me like sick fever. There I stood, my car fenced in by the Rolls-Royces and Bentleys of Hollywood royalty, while a woman I had grown to love was being driven away, to her death, by a lunatic FBI man.

I didn't have any choice! I had to steal a car.

"Forget it," I told the Negro, stuffing a sawbuck into his shirt pocket. "Just stay here for a few minutes. Grab a smoke."

I sprinted away.

"If you're going to put the arm on one," he called out, "bring it back before midnight."

As I turned the corner and ran toward the front of the house, a blue Cadillac was coming up the driveway.

Panting, I reached the car and leaned in through the front window. The driver, who had dipped his head to light a cigarette, turned to face me.

"What do you want?" asked Humphrey Bogart.

"Your car." It wasn't what I had planned to say, not at all, but confronted with Bogart, the truth rushed to my head like a snort of cocaine.

"What?" He was friendly, calm, a bit loaded.

"Why do you want the car?" asked his companion. She was thin and tawny, with sleek brown hair, large intelligent eyes, and a mouth you could have used for collateral. She was, I realized, Lauren Bacall.

"To prevent a murder," I said.

Bogart's mouth tightened. "You serious?" he asked.

"Very serious. Walter Adrian's widow is in terrible danger."

"Jesus Christ," said Bogart. He turned to Bacall. "Go inside, Betty, tell them I'll be late."

"I can't come?" she asked.

"No, no," Bogart grumbled. "C'mon, let this guy in the car. Helen Adrian. Christ almighty."

Bacall got out and I got in, thanking her profusely. She put her hands on the window, her eyes worried.

"Bogey, don't be a hero. Take care," she told him.

Bogart said not to worry, but we had to go; then he floored the gas pedal and sent us smoking out the driveway. He executed an impossible U-turn and went roaring up St. Cloud, which ran into Bel Air Road, and down a series of hair-raising curves to Sunset Boulevard. Bogart stopped at Sunset and turned to me.

"Which way and what's your name?"

I said I was Jack LeVine, a real-life detective hired by Adrian, then thought over where to go. It was some sweet decision to make because if I was wrong, I had let Helen slip out of my hands and out of this world.

"Santa Monica," I finally said. "Pacific Way."

"Pacific Way," the actor repeated. "That's a little north of Santa Monica." He bit lightly on his lip. "Okay, Chief, hang on."

He was a skinny man, actually, almost frail-looking, with thinning hair and deep hollows in his face. But for all that surprising physical delicacy, he was commanding, impressive, and a regular egg.

And he drove like a holy madman. Cigarette dangling from his lip, watching traffic with liquid brown eyes, occasionally taking a drink out of a flask of martinis, Bogart roared down Sunset Boulevard at an even seventy-five, running numerous lights in the name of chivalry.

"I heard about you," he said. "A New York detective, old school friend of Walter's; Larry Goldmark told me."

"We went to City College together."

Bogart chuckled deeply, the chuckle turning over into a cough.

"City College and you became a dick."

"Life has its little jokes."

"Ain't that the truth," the actor said. "I was supposed to be a doctor." His mouth tightened as he swerved to avoid a Buick that had just hit its brakes. "Who wants to kill Helen?"

"A guy."

Bogart groaned. "C'mon, Jack. I'm risking my neck driving like a drunk to get you there, you can at least tell me what's going on."

"I won't talk till it's over. You can understand that." I stuck a Lucky into the corner of my mouth.

"Shit," he said. "I've played shamuses. They blab like old women."

"That's in the movies."

He grinned.

"Everything's in the movies. That's all there is, movies. Doesn't America realize that yet?"

An ambulance cut us off as we headed down Burlingame to San Vincente Boulevard. It missed us by inches but Bogart didn't rattle. He was well-oiled but in full control, like any man comfortable with liquor. Booze was no opiate; it was fuel.

He lit a fresh cigarette with the butt of the old one, which snapped out his open window.

"The Carpenter murder," he said suddenly, turning to me, "the robbery story is bunk, right?"

"Right."

"I knew it. The day I read the story in the *Times* I told Betty it was a load of shit."

"His murder is connected to Adrian's murder, I'll tell you that much."

Bogart rubbed that chin.

"So those stories were true," he said slowly. "Walter didn't kill himself."

"He had no reason to."

"No?" The actor stared at me, his eyes curious and his hand slack on the wheel as we whipped up San Vincente at eighty miles an hour. I reflexively pointed in the direction of the windshield.

"Don't worry," he said placidly, ignoring the road, "I've done a hundred and ten with my head in an ice bucket."

"Why did you believe Walter was a suicide?" I asked him.

Bogart shrugged.

"The trouble he was having with Warners, the probability that the House Committee would be after him."

"But he's not the only one."

Bogart nodded, cigarette smoke streaming from his nostrils.

"Very true, Jack. They'll nail anyone who ever scratched his ass during the National Anthem. But some people just get worried; others might string themselves up."

"You worried?"

He fiddled with his bow tie.

"Anybody with half a brain is worried."

He hit the brake and we went off San Vincente at a modest sixty, running a stop sign, cutting a swath through a service station, and ending up on Route 1, the Palisades Beach Road.

"You said Pacific Way?" the actor asked.

"Check. I'm looking for a place on the beach."

"All right. That's about ten miles north of here." He smiled and stomped on the gas pedal. "Here we go."

Route 1 is a two-lane highway that runs alongside the sea. I've been told that it's quite scenic by day and positively dazzling the farther north you travel. But Route 1 twists and turns above that vast and turbulent ocean, and a person would not ordinarily think of doing one hundred miles per hour on it. But Bogart pushed the Caddy with quiet relish and made it seem unthinkable, unmanly, not to risk one's neck on this stretch of highway.

We began passing trailer trucks on the two-lane road, moving past them so quickly they seemed part of the landscape, like the houses and mountains and trees. It was a period of time, of motion, in which Bogart's life and my life were uninsurable, marked, doomed. And I enjoyed it, savored it even. The pursuit of a beautiful and good woman held captive by a two-time killer was the cleanest and simplest thing I had done in a long time.

And it crystallized to pure hunt, pure good and evil, when I saw the blue Nash proceeding at a modest pace about a hundred yards away.

"That's him," I told Bogart. "Slow down and put your brights on."

The actor effortlessly slowed us down to forty. While it felt as though we had stopped dead, we actually closed the gap between the two cars to maybe seventy-five feet. We were near enough to observe that only the driver was visible, his chunky figure planted solidly behind the steering wheel. My heart sank.

"Where's Mrs. Adrian?" asked Bogart. "And who's that driving?"

"We have to pass him," I said urgently. "I've got to see if she's in there."

"He'll notice us."

"He's going to notice us sooner or later anyhow. Let's move."

"You're the doctor." Bogart rubbed his jaw again and brought us up to a cruising speed of seventy. White checked his rear view mirror and noticed us closing in, but, the brights blinding him, had to turn away.

Bogart pulled out to pass the Nash. At that precise moment, a trailer truck no bigger than the U.S.S. *Missouri* came whining around a curve and loomed massively before us. Bogart floored the brake pedal and we went into a skid. Time stopped as the actor wrestled with the wheel, bringing the Caddy onto the road shoulder, spraying pebbles and whirling toward that dark and indifferent ocean. I watched the whitecaps as we spun closer to the edge, thought about my swimming. The spinning slowed and Bogart somehow brought us to a stop as the truck rumbled past, yellow lights blinking.

Time in.

"Very nice," I told Bogart. "Very, very nice."

He hitched his shoulders and tossed another butt out the window, then eased us back onto the road.

"We're going to pass this son of a bitch," he said briskly, "if it takes all night."

White was a few hundred yards away again, and picking up speed.

"I think he knows now," I said.

"That we're tailing him?"

"Yeah."

"Then I'd say we better catch him."

Within ten seconds, Bogart had stoked the Caddy up to ninety.

"This is some machine," I told him.

The actor merely nodded as we gained on the Nash. White had opened up to perhaps eighty. Bogart continued to accelerate and we hit a century.

"You can't do a hundred in a fucking Nash," he growled.

White tried, though. A race had developed, but the FBI man was outclassed. We hit a straight expanse of road and there was nothing but night on the southbound lane. Bogart pulled out to pass and drew to ten yards of the Nash. To five yards. We drew up to the rear of the car, which is when I saw the pair of trim legs horizontal on the back seat.

"That's Henry Perillo!" Bogart shouted.

At that moment Clarence White turned his head and faced us, his eyes peering myopically into the high beams. He shouted something, but I couldn't understand a word. Then he faced front. A second later, he whirled back and extended a revolver out his window.

"Down!" I screamed at Bogart. The actor ducked and braked the Caddy, but too late; the FBI man aimed carefully and sank one bullet into our right front tire. He fired at the left front, but he had lost his angle and missed. The Caddy rocked a bit but didn't skid. Limping like a great steel cripple, it came to an uneventful but frustrating stop at the side of the road.

"Goddamn it to hell!" I roared, banging my fist on the dash. Bogart was already out of the car and opening the trunk.

"C'mon, Jack!" he shouted. "Stop pissing and moaning; the son of a bitch could have shot out the radiator. Help me get this spare on."

It took no more than ten minutes to change the tire, but ten minutes can be an awfully long time. Bogart and I, stripped to our shirtsleeves, labored wordlessly in the cool, wet seaside air, communicating through grunts and pointed fingers. I hoisted the flat and dropped it into the trunk.

"A tough break," I said. "Maybe a fatal one."

"You pays your money and you takes your choice," the actor said, climbing into the driver's seat and starting the engine. "I'm telling you we'll catch him."

As fast as we drove, and the speedometer read 120 on one straightaway, we couldn't find the blue Nash.

"You still want Pacific Way?" Bogart asked.

"Yeah."

"Henry Perillo," he said contemplatively. "This is unbelievable. What's with him?"

"A lot. His real name is Clarence White and he's an

FBI man, undercover variety, who lost his cover and had to kill Adrian and Carpenter in order to regain it. The catch is that *he's* the one who's investigating the two murders—for the FBI. Pretty ingenious."

The actor turned to me and now there were tears in his eyes.

"Outrageous," he said softly and with difficulty. "It's horrible."

It was horrible all right. Unthinkable, bizarre, a bad dream. But here it was and here we were, pulling onto Pacific Way.

"I'll kill the lights," said Bogart.

At the end of the street I could see the three-story saltbox home, dark and desolate against a child's dream of a starry sky. The Nash was in the driveway.

"I'll get out here," I said. "Thanks for everything."

"Don't give me that crap," Bogart said, stopping the car and opening his door. "You're going to need help."

"You could get hurt. I only have one gun."

"Stop being a sap. Let's get going."

I got out of the car.

"All right," I told him. "But stay behind me and stay low."

"Don't worry." The actor grinned, suddenly filled with the giddy daring of the moment. "I've played this scene a hundred times."

We started up the road, jogging in a crouch, and we had gone maybe ten feet when we noticed the boat.

It was a cabin cruiser, about fifty feet long and anchored a few hundred yards out on the gently rolling ocean. At least two men were aboard making preparations for what appeared to be the start of a considerable journey. Barrels of gasoline were arranged in rows of three on the rear deck of the boat.

"That's an awful lot of gas," I said. "They're not just making a run up the coast."

"Looks like a couple of thousand miles worth," Bogart said quietly. "What do you think?"

"I think they're going to take Helen for a long ride."

"And Perillo—White you say his name is?—he stays here?"

"Yeah."

The actor ran his hand through his sparse hair and stared at the ground, then turned to me, pale and worried.

"You think she's alive?"

"White is very careful. I can't imagine he'd drive through Los Angeles with a dead woman in the back seat."

"Then how do we get her out of here?"

A very apt question. I folded my arms and looked up at the stars.

"Well," I began, "we obviously have to intercept him before he gets to the boat and we have to do it in such a way that those bozos out on the cruiser don't notice."

"He's bound to take her out in a launch, but there's none on the beach."

"So it's in the back of the house."

We looked at each other and nodded.

"I get into the boat," I told him. "Definitely."

The two of us continued loping up Pacific Way, hunched like marines about to hit a beachhead. I removed my Colt and held it tightly in my right hand. We reached the saltbox house and ducked down by the grill of the Nash.

"There he is," whispered the actor.

The bulky figure of White suddenly emerged from the rear of the house. He was carrying Helen in his arms and heading for the water. Her arms dangled loosely down to the sand and I detected—maybe wished into fact—an involuntary movement of her head.

"She's alive, Jack," Bogart said happily. "No doubt about it."

I simply nodded, watching in fascination as White awkwardly placed Helen down on the moonlit sand. He stared at her for a moment, as if suddenly struck by the fact of her beauty, then turned and walked back toward the house and out of view.

"The boat," I said. "He's getting the boat."

A minute later, White reappeared on the sand. He walked heavily and a rope was draped tautly over his shoulder. At the end of the rope was a small motorized boat, gliding smoothly over the sand.

"We have to act now, Jack," Bogart said, rising.

I held him down by the shoulder and got up myself, moving around to the door of the Nash and peering in through the window. The God in whom I believe at such moments had left the keys in the ignition. I scurried back to Bogart.

"We're in luck," I told him. "He left the keys in the buggy. If you get in and drive away, we might pull him off the beach. At the very least, it'll distract him."

"He'll shoot," the actor said. "Don't you think I need a gun?"

"No. Other people live on this beach. If White starts shooting, they'd come running out to see what's going on. That's the last thing he wants. He'd rather lose the car."

"Mebbe, mebbe not," said Bogart. "I'll give it a try."

The actor got up and slipped into the driver's seat of the Nash, bending down low over the wheel. I heard him feeling around. Suddenly he stuck his head out the window, delighted. He was holding a gun.

"Jack, look!" he whispered. "In the glove compartment."

"Take off!" I told him.

Bogart started the engine and turned on the headlights. He backed out of the driveway, honked, and started tearing down Pacific Way.

Clarence White, at that very moment lowering Helen's boneless form into the motorboat, looked up and gaped at the departing car. As he did so, I began running toward the right side of the house, stooped way down and heading away from his line of vision.

Things fell neatly into place, way too neatly. The FBI man, startled, dropped Helen into the boat and hurriedly left the beach. Bogart suddenly stopped the car. It was a shrewd move, serving to draw White on; he began racing toward Pacific Way. The actor fired a shot into the air, causing White to fling himself upon the ground. I saw him reach into his jacket pocket, at which point he realized that his gun was in the car.

While Bogart was toying with the undercover man, I made my way down to the beach, alternately watching White and the gentlemen on the cruiser. They were on the deck; one of them, I believe, was holding binoculars to his eyes.

Crab-like, I crawled along the sand and approached the boat, pulling myself over its side. I fell immediately to the wooden floor, belly down, and faced the beach with my gun drawn. Helen was curled on the floor against the stern of the boat, facing me, breathing with the measured heaviness of someone under ether. I made my way over to where she lay and examined her arm: there was a small puncture mark near the left elbow. I rolled her eyelids up; it was not pleasant to see those green and luminous eyes as dull and expressionless as those of a Boston scrod.

The taillights of the Nash shrank to red pinpoints down the road. White was running back from the road, looking concerned but unshaken. He entered the rear apartment of the saltbox house, turned on a light and walked around the kitchen. He moved out of range, into range, then out again. When he reappeared, he was holding a rifle. He pulled a short metal chain and extinguished the bare bulb. I ducked my head and listened as the door shut.

Helen groaned softly, her mind a drug-lit pinball machine. She had the sweats now; the lovely face and smoothly muscled arms were slick and wet, the red hair was turning to damp ringlets. It was chilly by the water and the lady could get a bad cold, but I resisted the impulse to drape my jacket across her body. Resisted it because White was walking quickly through the high grass around the house and was just now stepping onto the beach.

He was fifty yards from the boat.

I attempted to cover the situation. He had a rifle. That was to my advantage. While the rifle could easily blow the Holland Tunnel through my *kishkas,* it was clumsy to operate in a quick-draw, Wild-West situation. And this was the Wild West. You couldn't go farther west without getting wet.

Thirty-five yards.

I wanted to look up and get an exact reading on my angle to White, but couldn't do it, not even for a blurred instant, without revealing myself. If we started opening up at this distance, he had the goods on me. So I remained flat on my belly and waited.

Twenty-five yards.

I pulled my knees up a bit, gaining leverage and support. My nervous system, ganglia, pulse, and brain cells began to concentrate on that single connection between mind and right index finger. The waves pounded close behind and a spray of salty drops pelted my neck. Helen opened her eyes and although they appeared blank and uncomprehending, they saw something that made her scream.

It was a deafening, air-raid siren of a scream, a horrific noise at the worst possible moment. I heard White stop dead in his tracks and cock his rifle.

Helen screamed again, then abruptly closed her eyes and sailed back to her silent nightmare. Mine was just beginning. Between the Nash vanishing and the lady's howl, White had figured things out to the dime and demonstrated so by taking aim into the boat and missing my head by approximately one-quarter of an inch.

I stood up and fired at his approaching form, missing terribly. White quickly ripped off another salvo. It bit into my left shoulder and I tumbled over into the sand as two more shots, aimed from the cruiser, blew a hole into the motorboat.

I completed a somersault and came up to see White advancing on me, setting up a guaranteed jackpot at my skull. He was smiling. I took another tumble, straightening up and firing as I reached my feet. My potshot caught White in the wrist, opening a red geyser out of an artery and forcing his volley to fly in the general direction of the moon.

"Communist bastard!" White yelled at me. The arterial flow on his wrist continued unabated, but he quickly loosed a waist-high blast, Pretty Boy Floyd-style, that blew past my ear and out to sea. He was about to fire again when I killed him.

I don't enjoy killing people, but this was not a situation in which ethics were up for debate. It was caveman time and I got Clarence White with what was actually a bad shot. I wanted the heart, but the stinging pain in my shoulder was throwing off my balance, so the shot flew upwards and caught White below the Adam's apple, cutting his windpipe. He tossed his gun away and clutched at his throat, as if to repair the damage with his hands. Death broadcast a hoarse and ruined melody. It was no fun to hear.

I watched him die and almost got killed in the process. White's comrades on the boat started opening up and yet another bullet entered my left shoulder. Furiously, I grabbed at it, as if going after a wasp, and stumbled over to where White lay dead.

I took his rifle, then ran to the motorboat and pulled Helen out. She was unconscious but untouched by the gunfire. I turned the boat over and lay down on the sand beside it. My shoulder was bleeding badly and I could feel my head grow light. Four more shots flew past us. I set the rifle on the upturned bottom of the boat and fired out to sea, once, then again, but at best I might have wounded a careless squid.

A honking commenced to the rear. Bogart had returned in the Cadillac.

"Can you drive down here?" I shouted.

"Not in that sand," he hollered back. "We'll never get back out."

Another barrage from the cruiser drove me down. Bogart stepped from the car.

"Stay inside!" I yelled.

He pretended not to hear me and went running down the road, taking a position behind a rock. The men on the cruiser fired at his fleeting form, but missed. Bogart fired back, but the boat was well out of pistol range. It was a gallant gesture, but all it did was mark his position on the shore.

I peered through the rifle sight and held the stock as well as I could. Christ, how my shoulder hurt. I aimed at the gasoline barrels, invoked the spirits of Jehovah, Zeus, and DiMaggio, then pulled the trigger.

The back of the cruiser exploded in flames as instantaneously and violently as if I had bombed it from the air. The barrels were bunched closely together and the chain reaction of heat and combustible fuel literally blew the cruiser apart. Sections of wood and glass, and of arm and leg, were thrown over a thousand yards of ocean.

I stood up. Bogart stood up. The explosions continued; a fireball floated on the water like some biblical warning of doom.

People down the beach were crowding their decks and porches, watching the grotesque spectacle offshore.

"My shoulder," I called to Bogart. "Help me with Helen."

He came running down to the beach and I sat back down on the sand. Helen lay beside me, wet and motionless; I did not regret that she had missed the events of the past minutes.

Bogart knelt down and examined my shoulder.

"That's a beaut," he said. "Hurt like hell?"

"Yeah."

He bit his lip and took a handkerchief from his pocket, wrapping it around the shoulder and beneath the left armpit. The handkerchief was too small.

"Goddamn," Bogart said softly. He tossed off his jacket and undid his shirt.

"That's not necessary," I told him, my head spinning. "We can get to a doctor."

"Stop playing the hero," the actor said. He tied the dress shirt tightly around my shoulder. It rapidly turned red.

"I owe you a shirt," I said.

"Sure you do." He put his jacket back on over his tee shirt and looked at Helen.

"How is she?"

"Okay. Just junked up to the gills."

"The bastards," he said bitterly. The actor pointed at the dead form of Clarence White. "We leave him here or what?"

"We leave him here and call the cops."

"What are they going to do?"

"My guess is they'll report him missing."

"Then maybe we ought to make a stink. Bring him in ourselves."

I stood up to think it over, but the blood loss had taken its toll and I keeled over.

"The hell with it," Bogart said. "Let's get to a doctor."

He bent down and gently lifted Helen onto his back. This was a very splendid man. We started back to the Caddy. The trip took years and I began feeling nauseous. We reached the car and Bogart placed Helen down across the back seat, supporting her head with his jacket. I vomited by the side of the car, then got in.

Bogart was now attired in tee-shirt and slacks. He started down Pacific Way, driving away from the ocean.

People were standing in the road, talking in small excited groups. They turned and examined our approaching car; Bogart accelerated and blew right past them.

"Hey, listen," I said. "Thanks for everything."

"Anytime." The actor grinned. "Best Thursday night I've spent in weeks."

My stomach churned again. I closed my eyes and leaned my head back.

"Stop talking and relax, Jack," he said. "I don't want you puking all over the car."

We both laughed. I told Bogart he was one hell of a guy and he might have said that I was, too, but I passed out about then, so I'll never really know. I like to think he did.

14

Four evenings later, Helen and I boarded the Super Chief for the long trip east. We took a Pullman room and pulled down the shades. With the great Southwest a craggy moonscape outside our window, we indulged in long silences and a night of gentle, healing sex. It had been quite a fight and we both had our scars. Two bullets had been taken from my shattered left shoulder; a pin had been inserted, just temporary they told me, and the discomfort was considerable. As for Helen, it had taken her two days to emerge fully from the drugged coffin she had been nailed into. When her senses had cleared, she knew that she'd have to get away from Los Angeles.

We didn't talk about what had happened, at least not for a while. It was in the nature of a tacit agreement. There was a stopover in Albuquerque, a dozen hours out of L.A. It was 8:30 in the morning and we wandered out to have breakfast in the station coffee shop. Over hotcakes and sausage we spoke about little things—the trip so far, the extraordinary blue sky—and spent some warm and peaceful minutes just gazing out the window at the comings and goings on the platform.

Afterwards we strolled through the streets near the terminal. Helen bought an armload of authentic Navajo blankets from a silent, watchful Indian woman who looked to be in her seventies. Helen intended to deliver the blankets to her relatives in Utica.

"And one of them is for you, Jack."

"That's very kind," I said.

She shrugged, then smiled, then began to cry. The Indian woman stared straight ahead as the red-haired lady put that beautiful head on my good shoulder and let the tears flow.

"Christ," said Helen, "when am I going to stop crying?"

"When you don't feel like crying," I told her.

So she wept and we stood there, me and Helen and the Navajo blanket-seller, under that intensely blue sky in New Mexico, and if I had any brains at all, I would have told Helen to let the train go on without us.

Instead, I told her it was time to get back on. We reboarded slowly, reluctantly, and marched through the cars back to our room. Helen put the blankets away and blew her nose. She lit a cigarette, crossed her legs and looked out the window as the train started moving with that surprising first tug and we headed out toward the pastels of eastern New Mexico.

"We shouldn't have gotten back on the train," she said, facing the window.

"I was thinking the same thing. Beautiful out here."

She turned to me.

"So why didn't we stay?"

"Because I left my Luckies on the train."

She smiled an affectionate smile and took my hand.

"You're such a dumbbell." She kissed my fingers. "Is it immature of me to talk about doing that?"

"Maturity is highly overrated," I told her. "We didn't stay in Albuquerque because we just couldn't, that's all. We have responsibilities, debts, friends and relatives. All that crap."

206

"You don't think it has anything to do with maturity?"

"No, it has to do with vanity. How is the world going to function if we step off a train in New Mexico and disappear into the hills?"

"It could function without me," she said. "But I'm sure it couldn't without you." Helen rubbed my cheek. "You think the New York papers are going to run the story?"

I shrugged. We had avoided the subject until now, but there was no sense ducking it any further. It had been in the room with us since the beginning, doing its nails and yawning, waiting for us to acknowledge its troubling presence.

"*PM* might run it, but nobody else. Everybody's so scared now and the only evidence I have is that memo. But that's far from conclusive; any crackpot could steal some FBI letterhead for his own purposes."

"But it would take someone with knowledge to use the name of Clarence White," Helen insisted.

"Very true, except for one thing: Clarence White doesn't exist anymore. The FBI denies he was ever on the payroll —never heard of the guy, the Denver police have magically produced a death certificate for C. D. White, and P. J. Davis of the House Committee has left L.A. and nobody seems to know when he'll be back. It's what they call putting the lid on."

"What about the L.A. police?"

"They're covered. Walter killed himself, Carpenter was murdered by a robber—case as yet unsolved, and Henry Perillo and two unidentified companions perished in a boating accident. Too much fuel, someone lit a cigar."

"But Perillo, White, whatever his real name was—he had a bullet in his throat. How can they hide that?"

"Easy."

"And Lieutenant Wynn," I could hear the frustration in Helen's voice, "he knows what the real facts of the case are, doesn't he?"

"Unofficially yes. Officially, he doesn't know a thing. I let him read the White memo; he turned very pale and then told me that as far as he was concerned he'd never seen it."

"So that's it?"

"I'll keep plugging, but the climate right now . . ." I shook my head. "Nobody's going to believe a New York Jew detective over the FBI, the House Committee on Un-American Activities, and the L.A. police."

"But Bogart knows the whole story. He was an eyewitness."

"Bogart is a great movie star, but that's all. Against these powerhouses . . . hell, they'd ruin him. I can't let that happen." I filled my lungs with Lucky Strike. "I don't think anybody suspects how ugly this is going to get. Wynn said something."

"What?"

"Well, he's a smart cop, really. After he'd registered no sale on the White memo, I got up to leave but he told me to sit down. Then he lowered his voice to a peep and said that things were getting completely nuts and that for every White who got found out, there were a half-dozen others who would continue operating. Within six months, he said, a lot of people were going to be ratted on."

"What else did he say?"

"He asked me what I thought happened in the Adrian case."

Helen's nostrils flared in anger.

"Just out of idle curiosity?" she asked.

"Something like that."

"What did you tell him?"

"I leveled. No reason not to. I said White was the fifth column among the Hollywood Communists and his leverage at the Warners studio came from his having collared Parker when he was a Denver cop. Parker, needless to say, did not want a forgotten rape charge brought out for an airing, so when his old pal C. D. White—in his guise as Henry Perillo, boy Communist—arrived on the lot in 1943, he pulled all

208

kinds of strings to get him into the union and into a job. After that, whenever White wanted information, Parker gave it to him—about contracts, everything. And when White began feeling his oats, and when the climate was right, he forced Parker to put the screws on lefty writers. Walter was among the first."

"And nobody else knew about that old rape story?"

"Not that I know of."

Helen put her feet up on the empty seat beside me. The train barreled rhythmically along the roadbed, the double diesel engines whipping us past a horizonless sweep of mesas and cactus.

"What did Wynn say to all that?" Helen asked.

"He said 'uh-huh' a few times. Once he said 'mmn-mmn.' But the eyes gave him away; I know that he bought it."

"What did you tell him about Walter?"

"I admitted that I'd gone through the case believing that Walter had been murdered on the Western Street over a discovery that he had made, but that there were loose ends I couldn't tie up until the evening you suggested the possibility of an accident. That jelled it for me; it made sense of the note in Walter's pocket about checking the jailhouse. Suddenly the mystery blew clear; it was no mystery at all, just Fate, events. Walter was working late Monday night, got stuck trying to block out a scene and decided to visit the Western Street to help him visualize the thing. Left a note in case I showed up.

"He walked around the Western Street and eventually wandered into the jailhouse. There he found his buddy Henry Perillo hyphen Clarence White, flat on his back, dropping off some information into his little drawer. Walter was naturally curious and White panicked, went out of control. He cracked Walter on the head, knocked him out, then decided he might be able to get away with murder. So he carried Walter out to the gallows, which he had helped to build—I remember seeing the initials 'H.P.' on the underside of the scaffold—and made it look like suicide. He knew very well that people would believe Walter to be capable of taking his own life."

Helen had leaned her head back halfway through the story; she stared blankly at the baggage rack above my head. Now she folded her hands and looked toward me.

"What did Wynn say to all that?"

"Zippo. He doodled on his blotter and nodded. But he had to agree; there's simply no other explanation for Walter's death."

"Did he believe you about Carpenter?"

"It's all circumstantial, but it fits. The problem, of course, is that it hinges on a ridiculous circumstance, which is that both Carpenter and White had carried their written remarks to Walter's funeral in identical black leather slipcases. They rode out to the cemetery in the same limo. Sig Friedland was along, too. Naturally, they left the slipcases on the seat when they went to the gravesite, but White didn't want to leave his there, not at all. Friedland told me that he had started to carry it with him when the driver said 'Don't worry. It's safe here.' So he was stuck; he had to leave it."

"And they switched? I can't believe it. It's a bad movie."

"It is terribly corny, but it might have happened. Then again, it didn't have to be an accident."

"Dale did it on purpose?"

"Maybe. He wasn't an idiot. When White made a *megillah* about leaving the slipcase behind, he could have gotten curious and taken a gander inside. Friedland told me he was the first back in the car."

She smiled.

"You've been doing research."

"I had to do something while you were drying out."

Helen made a face.

"Meanie. So Dale looked inside the slipcase and saw the folder, correct?"

"Correct."

"Why was White carrying it around? It seems idiotic."

"Not only seems idiotic; it was idiotic. But he had a reason. Apparently White had taken the Parker folder—containing clippings, arrest sheets, the works—out of the jailhouse the night he killed Walter, figuring the cops might tear the place apart for one reason or another after the 'suicide.' Cops don't need much urging to tear a place apart; it's their only exercise, aside from lifting drunks, and who would know that better than an ex-cop like White? Anyhow, he intended to return the folder after the funeral because he didn't like to keep anything like that in his house. I went through his house and I know."

"So Dale saw the folder with the material on Parker and ran over to see him?"

"And White immediately figured out what had happened and sent his muscle over to stake out Parker's house."

"Which is where you got beaned."

"Which is where LeVine got beaned. The brilliant twist to remember, of course, is that by this time White had assumed command of the investigation of Walter's death and was spinning a Moscow assassination plot out of whole cloth. He had the L.A police stymied and the House Committee wallowing in every memo he wrote. It was pure genius."

Some Indian children waved at the train. They were coaxing a mule down a cracked and dusty road, but stopped to stare at the silver blur of passenger cars. I waved back and watched their forms recede.

"But why did he want to kill me, Jack?" Helen asked. "I didn't know a thing."

"I've been trying to get that straight in my head. There are a couple of explanations. One, he was looking for a scapegoat. He had murdered two people and was bright enough to realize that his usefulness as an undercover man was coming to an end. My guess is that after leaving that memo and killing you, he would have cleared out."

"So he just wanted someone to blame for the killings?"

"Sure. He had to nail someone for it. On top of that, he

might have suspected you had learned something from hanging around with me."

"But then why didn't he kill you?" She smiled as soon as the words were out. "I don't mean that he *should* have, Jack." Helen bit her lip. "It sounds awful every way I say it. You know what I mean."

"Sure I know what you mean: why didn't he just kill me and spare you? Well if you remember from our last broadcast, boys and girls, he did try and kill me. Twice. The first time when I started walking to the jailhouse the day after Walter's death—and that was an enormous mistake on his part because I was just wandering around in a state of blissful ignorance at that point. The shots let me know that Walter had definitely been murdered and that the jailhouse had something to do with something. Then, of course, he tried to finish me off on Pacific Way, but the hired help screwed that up."

"After which he figured you were unconquerable," Helen said with a wry smile.

"It was the logical conclusion. Anyhow, he had incriminated me in his memo as some kind of Commie minor domo and one-man goon squad. By the time I had finished kicking and screaming and trying to prove I was just another small-time shamus, he would have disappeared."

"If he had disappeared, you would have tracked him down, Jack. I know it." Helen leaned forward and stroked the hairs on the back of my hand. "You would have nailed him."

"Me and Bulldog Drummond." I tried to imagine C. D. White succeeding in tossing this lady to the sharks. "The man was evil. Not just crazy; flat-out evil. To insinuate yourself into a group of people like that, people whose politics were just a kind of self-righteous charade, for the express purpose of ruining them. . . ." My anger outran my eloquence. "It's fucking incredible."

Helen got up and tumbled gently on top of me, watchful

of my bum shoulder. The train crossed the Pecos River; two men on horseback stood on its banks. The West.

"It's over, Jack," she said, burying her head in my neck. "Let's try and forget about it. I know we won't, but let's try."

It's a long way home, past the silos and feed stores and water towers of the Midwest. A long dull way, but good for composing one's thoughts, for dulling edges that have grown too sharp. For a period of three and a half days, there is no place to go, no phone calls to make or take, no responsibility. It is a gift of time, a bonus, a ticket left unpunched.

The two of us did a lot of silent musing on that trip, watching the snowy countryside roll past, the winter light gray and unpromising. Helen would lean against my right shoulder, hooking her arm through mine, and we would stare into the monotony of Kansas and Missouri as if into a mirror. Little towns and main streets, cars lined up at crossings, school buses, appeared, disappeared, and reappeared, always the same.

In the evenings we ate leisurely meals in the dining car, the waiters graciously old-fashioned Negro men skilled at small talk and railroad stories. Patches of neon small-town night life—a movie breaking, a café—flew by. Reminders of a simple country. We ate, we watched, we listened to the conversation of other diners. Helen finally said what was on both our minds. She was drinking a whiskey sour as we rolled past some Missouri hamlet identified only by Van's Bar and Grill. It was just before dinner on Wednesday night.

"I feel as if we're holding this terrible secret," she said, "and no one out there knows."

"Do you think they'd care?"

She considered the question, playing with her swizzle stick.

"I don't know," she finally said. "But it's bound to affect them."

"I hope not," I said. "I'd like to think it was just a peculiar set of circumstances, just Hollywood, rather than a preview of things to come. If this Red hunt really gets moving, it'll take years to run out of gas. By then there's even going to be some nervous guys in Van's Bar and Grill."

It was snowing in Chicago when we switched to the Twentieth Century Limited late on Thursday afternoon. Snowing and cold, the damp cold that blows in off the lake and cuts through whatever you're wearing. Especially if you're wearing a raincoat with a cheap lining.

"You must be freezing," said Helen as we dashed along the platform.

I made the sign of the cross and Helen laughed. We boarded the train minutes before it pulled out, for the last disquieting leg of our journey home.

Friday. Dingy Pennsylvania skies and snow falling over acres of smokestacks and power plants. Helen and I had breakfast in our room, just coffee and buttered toast. The approaching arrival in New York was pinching our appetites and I knew why. Sure, we were nervous about trying to get the story of Walter and the FBI man into the papers but the real crunch was what to do about each other.

Helen planned to stay with me in Sunnyside for a few days before visiting her kin in Utica, at which point I would have to answer a barrage of questions from my curious neighbors: "Jack, who's the woman?" "Jack, what happened to the shoulder?" I'd fend them off and then go sit in my empty apartment, waiting for a call from Utica. The reality of a New York winter, of the set and dusty patterns of my life—apartment, subway, office—reassured and oppressed me all at once. I didn't know what the hell to do. At age forty I liked my little routines—my small-stakes poker games, my silent breakfasts and solemn perusal of the box scores—and after the mad week in California they loomed like mirages of peace and normality. Wasn't this woman nearly a stranger? What would I do with her?

And God only knows how many stews were boiling over in Helen's mind: Walter's murder, her own near-death, her sudden relationship with this bald detective, the upcoming visit to Utica. The lady's slate had been wiped clean in one week. So she held on to my arm for support and her grip grew tighter as we descended beneath Park Avenue for the final slow, dark miles to Grand Central.

We got up to organize our baggage, swaying as the train rocked ever so slightly. Helen looked so terribly nervous that I stopped what I was doing and went to hold her.

"God, Jack, what a couple of weeks."

"It's all gravy from here on in," I told her.

"You think so?"

I shrugged.

"What do I know. But I do know that you're my friend and that is a fine new event in my life."

Helen beamed.

"You're my friend, too, Jack. No matter what."

I think it was the "no matter what" that made us both feel a lot better. We smiled, relieved of the insane responsibility of "proving something" in the next couple of days. We were friends. We would always be friends, regardless of what else we might be to each other.

The train stopped. I tucked a small bag beneath my right armpit and picked up a suitcase. Helen took a valise in either hand.

"We'll flag down a redcap and then take a cab home," I told her.

"Okay, kiddo," Helen said happily. "You first, you're the cripple."

We got out of the train and delivered our luggage to a waiting porter. He followed as we made our way down the Twentieth Century's long red carpet. Ahead was the terminal. It was noon and thousands of people were crisscrossing the huge floor, cocking their heads to hear announcements, racing to catch trains and taxis and block-long limos, waiting to greet wives or mistresses or the deal of their lifetime. A blind woman played the accordion and a pair of nuns sat with open cigar boxes on their laps. It was bedlam and it was home. I took Helen's arm and steered her toward the door.